We Gon' Ride

Cobain & Keri

BY: ZAII

Chapter 1- Cobain

"Well, Well, Well, what do we have here?" I asked walking into the warehouse looking around at everyone.

"It's about time your bitch ass showed up," Ali yelled out.

I looked around and saw that nigga Bracka tied to the chair with a gunshot wound to the shoulder and his whole face fucked up.

"Dam y'all started the party without me I see," I said chuckling.

"We got bored waiting for you," Ali responded shrugging his shoulders as he wiped his hands on the towel that was on the table.

I pulled my shirt over my head and tossed it on the chair then grabbed my brass knuckles off the table then walked up on Bracka and stalled off on him and rocked his whole shit, I saw a few teeth fly out his mouth and he had a hole in his cheek.

"You thought you could steal from me and wouldn't nobody find out? Huh you bitch ass nigga," I yelled punching him again.

He spit some blood out his mouth as best he could and looked up at me and smiled at me with missing teeth and all.

"If you know I stole from you then I'm sure you know I had help, just think about it. Your operation is pretty solid so how would I be able to get in and out without nobody seeing me until now," He said making a valid point.

I turned and looked at Ali and we both looked around at everyone to see if anyone was missing from our group. It looked like everyone was in attendance, they knew we didn't play about disrespect or stealing, that was an automatic death sentence in our books. We ruled our camp with an iron fist and didn't play when it came to certain shit.

"Who helped you?" I questioned.

"That's going to cost ya. You want answers and I want to get out of here with my life," He reasoned.

"Is this nigga serious right now bro?" I asked Ali.

"Nah he can't be, like you stole a half a mill in product and you want me to spare your life? Nah that isn't happening so your best bet is to just tell me who helped you and I'll spare your families lives," I shrugged.

His eyes got wide and he looked at me trying to read if I was serious or not. Our motto is we don't kill women or children, but that didn't mean we didn't know people that did. He didn't have to know that though.

"If you feeling lucky try me," I responded.

"My family don't have shit to do with what's going on here," He spoke with attitude.

"That's where things seem to get a little sketchy, your family is a part of you. So, whatever you did we have to hold them accountable for also," I stated seriously.

He looked over at Ali and then back at me and put his head down, before picking it back up again with a smirk on his face then spoke.

"Man do what you have to do, them kids aint mine for one, for two my mom is a complete bitch and needs to die, and for three the nigga that helped me is dead and gone because if he could help me steal from you and you put him on then I can only imagine what he would do to me and my crew," He spoke calmly.

I looked around at my crew again making eye contact with everyone and that's when it finally hit me that Rahim was missing. I looked and made eye contact with Ali and mouthed Rahim's name. He put his head down and shook his head, I knew that one hurt him since that was his little man and he was grooming him to be a future boss. Niggas never want to wait until it's their turn to shine and always get greedy and fuck themselves up. I was pissed off that he wasn't here anymore so I could kill him myself.

"So, since you aren't scared of death you ready to go now then fuck boy?" I asked pulling out my gun and aiming it at him.

"Wait before you pull the trigger bro, where's our product?" Ali quizzed him.

"Some of it has been repackaged and sold as our work and the rest of it is put up for safe keeping," He casually spoke.

If I wasn't trying to kill him I would salute him for being tough as he was. He wasn't scared to die and I admired that shit, but today wasn't the day for to me to be giving out Grammy's or acknowledgment's.

"Man kill this nigga, he isn't talking shit that we want to hear," Ali barked out.

"If you kill me, you won't get your product back. Isn't that what all this is about? Your product?" He egged on as best he could.

"Your ass is dam near dead anyway look at you, so whether or not I kill you your good as dead anyway," I shrugged not really giving a fuck anyway.

"Now since I'm as you say dam near dead, let me offer you a proposition. Let me go as is or you can suffer a terrible fate," He stated.

"What in the entire fuck are you talking about?" Ali barked.

As soon as he said that we saw one of our men drop to the floor with a single gunshot wound to the head. We all pulled our guns out and looked around to see where it came from.

"Who was that?" I yelled out pointing my gun at him.

"That was my partner who doesn't take kindly to me being here under these circumstances, so unless you want your whole crew's death on your hands. I suggest you let me go," He stated with a half grin.

"How did they even know where we were, this place is in the middle of nowhere," Ali spoke still looking around just as another one of our guys were hit causing my guys to start shooting all around.

    Once the smoke cleared we all looked around and Bracka was still sitting there with a smile on his face showing his missing teeth.

    "How did they know you were here?" Ali asked again still holding his gun and looking around.

    "Come take a look at my belt," He said smirking.

    I walked over to him and looked at his belt, I didn't see shit so I started getting more pissed off.

    "Man, what's with this belt, you are tempting me right now and I'm about to put a bullet in your skull" I threatened.

    "Look closer, open up my buckle," He spoke.

    I opened his buckle and I'll be dammed if it wasn't a tracking device in it, and that's when it all happened the door was kicked opened and everything was erupted in gunfire. I ran and hid behind a wall and started busting shots at whoever was coming my way. I looked over to see if I could see Ali and that he was good when I saw him peak up from behind the couch and shoot someone right in the head that was sneaking up on him.

"You good?" I called out from behind the wall.

"Yeah," I replied still shooting around me.

I looked around the wall and continued to shoot, Bracka's men never stopped coming in and by now we were outnumbered. I looked around and saw most of my men down. I open my chamber and saw I only had two shots left, and way more men. I looked from behind the wall and made eye contact with Ali and told him to cover me, I was going to try and get by him so we could try and make a run for it before we get ourselves killed.

I saw Bracka dead still tied to the chair, so I already knew this wasn't going to be a good thing for us. I signaled Ali and told him to cover for me on three, I took one more quick look around the wall and took a deep breath and made the way to Ali. I ran as fast as I could as Ali stood from behind the couch and covered me. I let off my two shots and he was shooting what he had as I was running.

"AHHHHHHHHHHH" I yelled out just as I made it to the couch.

"Fuck bro what happened? Were you hit?" Ali asked dropping down beside me as he emptied his clip and refilled it.

"Yeah," I spoke through clenched teeth and labored breaths.

"Shit, we gotta get out of here, this my last round. So, I say we make a run for it," He spoke.

I laid there in pain taking deep breaths trying to control my breathing, in all the time that I've been in this game I never managed to get shot. This shit hurts like a bitch.

"Cobain, we have to get you out of here. Do you hear me?" He quizzed.

I shook my head up and down acknowledging what he was saying. I was starting to feel weak but I knew what he was saying was right and I wasn't going to die here I had a daughter that needed me. I looked around as best I could to see if there was a way that we could get out of here.

"Look we don't have that much time, shoot the lights out then the alarm, then we can probably try and make it to the office. It sounds like they are running out of ammunition, we got most of them but not them all.

"Aight," Ali responded.

I laid there trying to block out all the pain that I was feeling right now so that we could make it out of here in one piece.

"You ready?" Ali asked looking at me.

"Yeah," I replied.

I took some breaths and prepared myself for what was about to come. I knew if we could make it to our office we had a great chance of escaping. Our office was bulletproofed and we had a secret door that led to an ally outside.

Ali stood up and shot the main light making the whole warehouse pitched black and I got up and we both made a run for it. Ali was still shooting at anything he could being that we couldn't see. Once in the office he closed the door, and pulled the shades down so nobody would see our moves.

"Shit, man everything is fucked up right now," Ali said as he came and looked at my wound. He looked around trying to find something, then when he opened the closet he pulled out a long sleeve shirt and wrapped it around me as best as he could to try and control the bleeding.

"Sssssssssss," I moaned out when he tightened it.

"My fault bro, but I had to do that. We are getting out of here," He assured.

We heard the bullets hitting the door but we weren't worried about them getting in. Ali moved the file cabinet over an appeared the door that we had put there for emergencies. After he did that he opened the draw and pulled out another gun and some more bullets. Ali then opened the door then came and helped me up and we made our way out the door.

We had to walk through this tunnel before we could make it to the ally, he was holding me up as we made our way through.

"Don't worry bro, I got you," He stated.

I didn't even reply but I knew he did it was always us for a long as I could remember. By the time we made it to the door a nigga was beyond tired and just wanted to sleep. Ali opened the door and moved as quickly as he could to get us from out the ally and to the car.

"Fuck where's the car?" Ali barked out of breath when we made it to where the car was supposed to be.

"Shit," I mumbled.

"Hold on, bro. I got you," He responded.

Ali picked me up from against the wall and made his way to the end of the ally, as soon as we got near the end we head a bunch of noise. Ali turned and looked behind us and saw Dragon behind us with his army.

"WERE YOU GOING SOMEWHERE FELLAS?" Dragon called out.

"Fuckkkkkkkk, this can't be happening right now," Ali barked out.

I was getting weaker and weaker and didn't know how much more I had in me. I was feeling lightheaded by now.

"Listen to me bro, I'm going to try and hold them off as long as I can I need for you get out of here and I will catch up with you," He told me.

"No, I'm not leaving you," I spoke through my teeth.

"Right now, isn't the time for this shit Cobain, I told you I got you and I do. I promise I'm good, but I can't do much with you right here injured," He stated.

I looked at him not really knowing what to say, I wasn't comfortable leaving him here alone to fight all them niggas off but I knew I wasn't in the right shape to help him let alone help myself.

"Trust me," He said looking me in the eyes.

I nodded my head up and down, I trusted him he was a sniper when it came to busting his guns he never shot his gun and missed a target.

"On the count of three I'm going to need to get the fuck out of here as fast as you can, I'm going to cover you.

"Okay," I responded.

"Don't worry, I'm going to see you in a few," He smirked.

I nodded at him and waited for the count.

"One," He started.

I leaned up on the wall and pushed all that pain to the back and prepared to get out of here with my life. I took a deep breath and waited for him to hit three.

"Three," He yelled and started shooting at the men behind us.

I took off as fast as I could out the ally, I made it and ran down a street and didn't see anyone outside. I tried to act normal as best as I could but it wasn't working a nigga was starting to bleed out. As I got a little further down the street I dropped to my knees and started to crawl.

The pain was starting to become unbearable and I was slowly losing consciousness, I tried to pull my phone out my pocket and call for help but it became too much and I ended up dropping it beside me. I wasn't trying to die out here in the streets alone like I was a nobody. I crawled until I couldn't anymore, and I just laid. I was tired and didn't have any more fight left in me. I laid there and thought about my baby girl, the only thing in life I ever got right. Seeing her pretty face flash before my eyes gave me a boost of strength, I pushed myself to crawl a little further until I heard these voices. I crawled a little further until I couldn't anymore and I just stopped and tried to control my breathing.

I closed my eyes and said a prayer up to god to watch over my daughter.

"OH MY GOD CREE" I heard a female voice yell.

I opened my eyes again and swore I saw an angel from up above.

The only thing I could get out my mouth before it all went black was.

"Please don't let me die,"

Chapter 2- Keri

"OH MY GOD CREE," I yelled out looking around at my surroundings.

"What in the entire fuck is going on?" She responded.

I quickly pulled off my jacket and applied pressure onto the gunshot wound so this man wouldn't bleed out more then he already has.

"Cree call 911," I shouted.

"Come on sir stay with me, don't leave just yet," I tried to coach.

I looked behind me and saw Cree on the phone giving out our location, I could only hope this man had more time left. I felt his pulse and it was getting weaker, so I knew he didn't have much time left. I kept the pressure applied to the wound as best as I could, but I couldn't help but notice how handsome he was. I wonder what he was doing to land himself in this situation.

"Keri their here" I heard Cree say bringing me from my thoughts of him.

"Okay, perfect," I responded. I didn't remove my hands from his wound until I felt the EMT come beside me and takeover.

"What happened ma'am?" The EMT asked.

"My friend and I were walking and saw this man lying here like this, so I applied pressure to the gunshot as I told my friend to call you guys. I check and his pulse is slow, about 25 beats per minute." I stated.

I watched as they inserted an IV in his arm then placed him on a stretcher and then lifted him into the ambulance.

"Are you riding with him?" He asked me.

I looked over at Cree and she touched my shoulder and smiled, giving me the okay.

"Yes, I am," I replied getting into the back.

"What hospital?" Cree called out.

"Jamaica Hospital," The EMT called out closing the door.

I saw Cree run towards the car so she could follow behind us to the hospital. I closed my eyes and said a silent prayer to the man up above that this handsome stranger wakes up soon, because with all this blood lose I don't know if he was even going to be able to survive this.

The EMT cut open his shirt and started working on him as we rode to the hospital, but it wasn't looking good. His heartbeat was dropping, and dropping fast. That's when we heard the beeping sound, he flatlined right there in the back of the truck. I quickly jumped into action and started doing CPR on him.

"Grab the AED and open it so we can shock his heart while I'm doing this," I ordered.

He looked at me like I had some nerve telling him what to do in his truck, but we had a man's life to save.

"I'm Dr. Keri Alexander, now if you want to save this man's life I suggest you do as I say," I said in a stern voice.

He turned and grabbed the AED kit from the shelf behind him and opened it and put each side on his chest, as I still performed CPR on him.

"Clear," He yelled.

I removed my hands from his chest and watched as the electric current went through his body. I looked over at the monitor and he was still flatlined, I continued doing CPR again as he got ready to shock him again.

"CLEAR" He yelled.

Again, I watched as his body was jolted with electricity we both looked over at the monitor again and slowly we saw a heartbeat rhythm again.

"Thank god," I whispered to myself.

By this time, we were pulling into Jamaica hospital emergency room, the EMT grabbed the IV bag and placed it on his chest and prepared to bring him out the truck. They got him out the truck and wheeled him inside where the doctors were waiting for him. They took him from the EMT's and wheeled him straight to the back for surgery.

I stood there watching and praying as the doors closed and he was gone. As I turned to go to the waiting area Cree was coming in and she met me and I ran into her arms and just cried. I don't know why I was crying, I didn't even know this man but it still scared me because he almost died and since I've been a doctor I have been lucky to never lose a patient and even though he wasn't mine I felt like he was.

"Come on let's go sit down," Cree whispered.

I nodded my head up and down as she led the way to waiting area so we could wait to see if that stranger made it or not.

"We need to get you cleaned up, do you have any change of clothes in your locker?" Cree asked.

"I'm… I'm not sure," I responded in a low tone.

"Look I know a lot happened today but I'm going to need for you to snap out of it, I'm sure he's going to be okay and I'm pretty dam sure it's because of you," She spoke with a smile.

"Yeah, you're right thank you," I replied hugging her.

I stood up and told Cree I would be right back I went to the locker room to check if I had any more clothes in my locker to change into since I was covered in blood. Once I was there I opened my locker and saw a picture of my fiancé Max and I, from happier times. I overlooked the picture and pulled out a pair of blue jeans and a shirt that I could change into. I laid it on the bench and went to the bathroom and washed my hands to get the dried-up blood off me. Once I dried my hands I went back into the locker room and took off my clothes and placed them all in a garbage bag and put on my clean clothes. I tied the bag up and placed it in the trash can before closing my locker and leaving out the locker room.

 I made it back to Cree and saw that she was still sitting in the waiting area alone.

 "Anything yet?" I asked getting impatient.

 "Nope but shit you a doctor here I'm sure you can find out what's going on," She pointed out.

 "That's true, thanks girl," I laughed.

Soon as I was about to get up I heard a cell phone ringing, I pulled mine out and checked it. it wasn't mine.

"Cree you phone ringing?" I told her about to walk away.

"Nah boo mine on vibrate so it definitely isn't mine," She said.

"So, who phone ringing?" I questioned.

"Oh shit, I forgot that when I was going to get the car I found a cell that was a little away from him," Cree remembered.

She pulled the phone from her bag and looked at it, and sure enough it was someone calling that man's phone.

"Pick it up," I told her.

"Hell no I don't know that man," She said trying to hand me the phone just as it stopped ringing.

"You're so childish it could be his family looking for him," I stated.

"Well if it is YOU can deliver the bad news that's what you get paid the big bucks for anyway," She shrugged.

Just as I was about to say something the phone rang again and I jumped a little because it scared me.

"What does it say?" Cree asked.

"It just says A," I replied.

"Well hurry up and pick up before A hangs up again," She urged.

I sat down next to her and put the phone on speaker as I answered it, before I could get a word out I heard a man's voice blaring through the speaker.

"Ayo bro, you good? Where you at? Yo, Cobain," He called out.

So, Cobain is that guy's name, so mysterious, just like him.

"HELLOOOOOOO," He yelled out snatching me from my daydream.

"Oh sorry, hello... hello," I spoke up.

"Who the hell is this and where is my brother?" He asked sounding pissed off.

"I'm Keri and my best friend and I found your brother laying on the sidewalk half dead," I told him.

"WHERE IS HE? IS HE ALIVE?" He rambled off.

"He's stable, I'm a doctor and was able to help the EMT stabilize him," I stated.

"Where are you at now?" He asked sounding impatient.

"We are at Jamaica hospital," I responded.

"Bet," Was all he said.

I looked at the phone and sure enough he hung up on me, which probably meant he was on his way here.

"Well that was rude," Cree spoke.

"I'm used to it, let's go to the cafeteria, I need a coffee bad," I joked.

We got up and went to the cafeteria so I could get me a coffee and something sweet because I had a feeling this was going to be a long night.

We came back upstairs with our stuff just as a man was walking into the waiting area. He was very good looking, he was brown skin and covered in tattoos and had shoulder length dreads that were neatly done. He was soft on the eyes, he pulled out a cell phone and pressed a button then placed the phone to his ear. Just then the man who name I found out was Cobain his phone began to ring in my pocket.

He looked over at me and we locked eyes and he walked over to us and stood in front of me.

"Are you Keri?" He asked.

"Yes, and this is my sister Cree," I introduced.

He looked over at her and it was like his eyes got stuck on her, I don't blame him either because Cree was beautiful and had the most amazing chocolate complexion ever. You would have thought he found love at first sight, but just that quick the look disappeared.

"I'm Ali, now what happened to my brother?" He asked switching into someone else that quick.

"Well as I said before he was stable when we got him here, we are just waiting to hear back from the doctor. They took him to the back for surgery," I told him.

"Whew, thank god," I heard him say as he ran his hands down his face.

He sat down in the chair and laid his head back against the wall, he looked like he had the whole world on his shoulders and was stressed beyond anything we could do for him.

"I'm pretty sure your brother is fine, I'm a doctor here and we take pretty good care of our patient's here I promise," I told him as I tried to reassure him and myself.

The doctors have been back there a long time now and this wasn't like them, usually they come and give the family an update or something.

Just as he sat up and was about to talk the doctors finally came in.

"Dr. Alexander," He greeted

"Dr. Jones," I responded back.

"Are you kin to the man in the back?" He questioned.

"No, I found him, and rode in the ambulance with him," I told him.

"Oh yes the EMT said that, your actions might have saved this man's life," He acknowledged.

"I was just doing my job, this is his brother. How is he?" I inquired.

"Well sir your brother made it out of surgery, we were able to remove the bullet. We had to place him in a medically induced coma to help his body heal faster without all the pain. He also lost a lot of blood so we had to give him a blood transfusion to level him out," Dr. Jones explained.

"But he will make it right?" His brother asked.

"Yes… yes, he will," He responded with a smile.

"Thanks doc," He replied holding his hand out to shake.

"Once we are done we are going to have him moved then you can see him," He spoke while shaking his hand.

I took a deep breath and thank god for sparing that man's life tonight.

"Well now that you're here me and Cree are going to head on home, here's his phone," I spoke handing him the cell.

"Yo real shit thanks for everything, I owe you. If it wasn't for you my brother wouldn't even be here right now. So, if there's anything that you need don't hesitate to ask," He spoke sounding so sincere.

"No, its fine I promise. I was just doing a good deed," I assured.

"Well take my number in case you think of something, and my name is Ali," He finally introduced.

"I'm sure I won't think of anything but okay," I responded handing him my phone.

He put his number in my phone then handed it back to me, then turned to Cree and smirked at her.

"To bad we had to meet under these circumstances, but I hope I can see you again," He said picking up her hand.

"It is, but you probably won't. I'm glad your brother is okay, have a goodnight," She spoke walking away.

"Excuse her, it's been a long night," I told him.

"No sweat, right now isn't the right time anyway once it is she will know," He said in a confident tone.

As I was about to respond I saw the cops heading our way, so I knew whatever this was far from over.

"You have company," I whispered.

He turned and looked behind him and instantly got annoyed, I saw it all in his face.

"Thanks again, get out if here and don't forget to let me know if you need anything," He spoke.

I walked away just as the cops were coming to question him for I'm pretty sure tonight's activities. I walked outside and saw Cree leaning up against the car waiting for me.

"Girl why you play him to the left like that?" I asked laughing.

"First off you know I don't date drug dealers, and I'm not finna get caught up in whatever mess he has going on," She stated.

"First off how you know he's a drug dealer and for two how you know he got shit going on?" I questioned.

"Girl do I look like boo boo the fool to you, if he doesn't have anything going on he does now that his brother got shot, and second he has drug dealer written all him," She stated in a matter of fact tone as she got in the car.

"I guess you're right," I admitted.

"Don't guess, I am right. I always am," She joked sticking her tongue out at me.

We got in the car and continued talking about our night and the guys who invaded it.

***

When I got to my house I shut my car off and put my head on my steering wheel, today was a long day. I couldn't wait to get in the house and take a shower, my body was tired and I couldn't wait to lay down. I'm happy Cree and I were at the right place at the right time and could save a life tonight.

I grabbed my purse out the passenger side of the car and stepped out my car and made my way to my house. I pulled my keys out and opened my door letting myself in the house, I closed the door behind me and went straight to my room. I opened my bedroom door and went straight into the bathroom and started the shower, while the bathroom was heating up I walked into my closet and started to strip out of my clothes.

"Why are you coming home so late?" Max asked from behind me startling me.

"I… I was at the hospital with Cree," I told him.

I saw the glass of liquor in his hand so I already knew this situation wasn't going to be a good one. Whenever he got drunk he turned into a different person.

"Why are you stuttering dear?" He asked in a patronizing tone.

"You just caught me off guard," I told him honestly.

I continued taking off my clothes then grabbed my towel and wrapped it around myself and continued to walk pass him and head back to the bathroom, until he grabbed me by my arm and stopped me.

"How did you end up at the hospital with a different pair of clothes on if you went out for dinner and a movie with Cree?" He asked through clenched teeth squeezing my arm.

"Owwww your hurting me Max," I yelled out in pain.

"Answer my question then dear," He said squeezing harder.

"Ahhhhhhh, we did go out and on our way to the car we saw a man on the ground bleeding out so I did what I could do to save him until the ambulance came. You're hurting me Max" I yelled with tears coming from my eyes.

He continued to squeeze my arm and stare at me until he finally let me go and turned and walked away leaving me in pain in the closet. I stood there crying silently to myself for a few minutes until I got myself together enough to go take a shower. I walked out the closet and headed straight to the bathroom.

"KERI," Max called out.

I took a breath wiped my tears and opened the bathroom door to see what he wanted.

"Yes," I replied.

"Come here," He summoned.

I walked over to where he was sitting on the bed and stood in front of him and waited to see what he wanted to say.

"So, if you were really at the hospital like you said you was, then you don't have an issue with me smelling your pussy, right?" He asked in a sadistic tone.

"Are you for real right now Max? Smell my pussy for what, that's Ludacris," I told him and walked away.

I got halfway to the bathroom and I felt myself being swung around and that's when I felt his hand across my face then I was dropped to the floor.

"YOU WILL DO WHATEVER THE FUCK I TELL YOU TO KERI, DO YOU FUCKIN' UNERSTAND ME?" He yelled.

"Yes… yes Max," I stammered.

"GOOD, NOW GET THE FUCK UP AND GET YOUR ASS ON THE BED SO I CAN SMELL YOUR FUCKIN PUSSY, AND DON'T MAKE ME SAY IT AGAIN OR THAT SLAP WILL BE THE WORSE OF YOUR PROBLEMS," He continued to yell.

"Okay, okay," I responded quickly getting up and getting on the bed.

"That a girl, now spread em" He said with a smirk.

He drank the rest of his drink then dropped the cup on the floor shattering it, then placed his hands on my legs and caressed them before forcing them open more then I already had them. He licked his lips then slowly lowered his head in between my legs and took a whiff of my pussy, then next thing I felt his cold wet tongue lick me from slit to slit. I just laid there not moving or saying anything at all. After he licked it he then kissed it and stood up.

"That's my girl, and she's wet just like I like her. Go shower so I can get some of my pussy. You got my dick hard as fuck right now" He said smiling at me holding his dick.

I quickly hurried up and ran into the bathroom and shut the door and just broke down crying. This wasn't how I pictured my life to be when I said yes to being his wife, it's like as soon as I said yes shit with us changed. I really don't know how much more of this I was going to be able to take.

"HURRY THE HELL UP IN THERE," He yelled throwing something at the door.

I got up from off the door and jumped in the shower that was still running, I silently cried from the pits of my soul. This life I was living wasn't my own and I didn't know how I was going to escape it. I grabbed my loofa and started to wash my body, my tears wouldn't stop falling. I felt like I was trapped and needed a way out.

"TIME'S UP KERI," He spoke opening the bathroom door causing me to jump.

"Coming," I said in a low whisper.

I washed off then got shut the water off and grabbed my towel and wrapped it around me then stepped out the shower. I looked at my reflection in the mirror and I looked tired, my eyes went to my arm and I saw that I had a bruise from where he grabbed me. I knew I was going to have to cover yet another bruise. I cut on the sink and grabbed my toothbrush and brushed my teeth, once that was done I took a deep breath and walked out the bathroom to see Max laying on the bed waiting for me.

"Let's go," He commanded.

I walked over to the bed and went to my side of the bed, I dropped the towel and got in the bed. I laid there and controlled my breathing, I didn't want to upset him anymore than he already was. He got out the bed and went to the mini bar we had in the corner of the room and took another shot of whatever we had back there.

He dropped his boxers right there and started stroking his dick right there while never taking his eyes off me. He slowly made his way over to me, when he got to me he stood there still stroking his dick with a smirk on his face. He climbed on top of me spreading my legs apart with his.

"You know you want this," He slurred.

I held my breath and waited for him to enter me, if this is what the rest of my life consisted of you could just kill me now. All I could do was lay here and wait until he was done with his business so I could go to sleep.

Chapter 3- Ali

Dealing with them cops all night was a fuckin' hassle but one call to the commissioner put an end to all them and their fuckin questions. Now that I knew my nigga was out the woods I was happy as a motherfucker, it was all up to him now to wake up. I was impatiently waiting we had shit to do and I wasn't going to feel safe while I'm out in these streets and he was in here laid up alone.

I pulled up to Cobain's baby mama house to drop off some money for her, shorty was a nag and that's putting it politely but I'll give her one thing she was a good ass mom to his daughter Kaylee. I got out the car and walked up to the door and rang the bell, I had a key that Cobain gave me for emergencies but I was going to respect her privacy unless I felt shit was different. I waited for a few minutes before I finally heard the door open, I looked down and saw Kaylee open the door.

"Hiiiii uncle Ali," Kaylee beamed.

"Hey princess, what are you doing opening the door without asking who it was?" I questioned whole giving her a stern look.

"I looked out the window and I saw your car, so I knew it was you," She stated.

"But baby girl I'm not the only one in the world with this car, it could have been anyone at the door, so you have to always make sure you ask who it is for your own safety," I explained.

"Sorry uncle Ali," She said lowering her head.

"Don't be sorry baby girl, just be smart. You lucky it was me and not your daddy, you know he would have gotten you right?" I quizzed.

"Yes," She replied pouting.

"Good, don't worry this will be our little secret," I whispered in her ear as I hugged her.

"Thank you," She smiled.

"Where's your mom?" I questioned.

"She's upstairs on the phone," She told me.

I instantly got mad, usually she's on her shit with stuff like this we've been down here for about five minutes talking, and she hasn't not once came and checked to see who was at the door, shit like this pissed me off. Especially since shit with Cobain popped off Kaylee ass could have been long gone by now.

"Okay, go sit in the living room I'm going to go talk to your mom," I told her putting her down.

I closed the door behind me then went upstairs to her room, I stuck my ear to the door and made sure I didn't hear another nigga in there. Shyne was stupid but I don't think she was that stupid, when I didn't hear nothing I opened the door and saw her laying across the bed on the phone. I walked over to her and grabbed the phone out her hands.

"What the- "She started to say.

"What the fuck is right, what the fuck are you doing up here on the phone while your six-year-old daughter answers the door huh Shyne? Then to make matters worse we've been down there talking for a good ten minutes and you didn't come check to see what the fuck was up," I snarled.

"She wouldn't answer the door without telling me she knows better," She responded.

"Hell yeah she does but she saw my car and let me in, I could have been anyone then she would have either been dead or kidnapped and your ass up here on the phone like you the got dam queen of Sheba," I yelled.

I didn't mean to yell at her but I didn't play when it came to Kaylee's safety at all and she knows that, if it was Cobain he probably would have hung her stupid ass out the window.

"You right, I'm slipping my fault Ali," She apologized.

"You dam right you are, listen it's some shit going on so I'm going to need for you to be on point," I told her straight up.

"What's going on?" She asked.

"Listen I can't tell you right now,"

"Where's Cobain I've been calling him all night," She asked.

I took a breath and ran my hands down my face, I really wasn't trying to tell her shit but I didn't have much of a choice.

"ALI," She shouted.

"Okay dam chill, he's in the hospital he got shot, and he's in a coma" I told her.

She looked like she just lost her best friend she dropped down to her knees and started crying. I didn't know what to do to console her so I just started patting her back like she was my Pitbull.

"Man get up, you have to be strong, he's fine trust me," I assured her.

"I need to go see him," She said as she got up and ran in her closet to get her sneakers.

"SHYNE CHILL," I barked.

I looked behind me to make sur Kaylee wasn't coming up the stairs and could hear us.

"Listen I really need for you to chill and let me handle this, once he's clear to be moved I'll send someone for you so you can go see him. Right now, I need you to relax and figure out what you are going to tell Kaylee when she asks for him," I explained.

She nodded her head up and down like she understood but I know this was hard for her to take in right now, hell I'm still not believing it myself.

"Just pray and stay strong, I got this," I assured her.

I went in my pocket and pulled out some money and handed it to her, before I turned to walk out the bedroom.

"I have his phone so if you need anything just call me," I told her.

"Okay," She replied.

I went back downstairs and sat in the living room with Kaylee for a minute.

"Listen baby girl, I need you to do me a favor," I told her putting her on my lap.

"Okay uncle Ali, anything for you" She said with a smile on her face.

"I need you to go upstairs and hug mommy she's sad and a hug from you will make it all better," I told her.

"Aww why is she sad?" She asked in a concerned tone of voice.

"She just got some bad news but she will be okay, I promise," I assured her.

"Okay I'll give mommy a lot of hugs then," She spoke.

"That's good, she would like that" I told her.

I reached in my pocket and pulled out a twenty and handed it to her.

"What's this for?" She inquired.

"After you give mommy a lot of hugs ask her can you take her to get ice cream," I suggested.

"But I can't drive uncle Ali," She giggled.

"Obviously smart girl, she drives and you can pay to make her feel better," I told her.

"OOOO OK, got it, I can do that," She assured me.

"Perfect princess, I'm going to get out of here but I'll come see you later," I said putting her back down on the couch.

"Uncle Ali," She called out.

"What's up princess," I turned and looked at her.

"Can you tell my daddy to call me please," She said with a smile.

"I will princess," I told her and quickly walked out the house.

I jumped in my car and just sat there for a minute I needed to go check on Cobain but a nigga was tired and literally only workin' on three hours of sleep. I decided to call up to the hospital and make sure everything him was good and just take my ass home to sleep for a few hours then start up again. I sent one of my young niggas up to the hospital to sit with him until I was able to get back up there.

I pulled off and headed to my house, I stopped by the Jamaican restaurant and picked me up something to eat then went straight to the crib. I got to my place shut the engine off and hopped out. I walked to my door and hit the security code and let myself in, I walked straight to the living room cut on the television and sat down and dived into my food.

Soul Plane was on and I was cracking up, no matter how many times I watched this it would be forever funny to me. I don't care how old it was, I put the plate down and cracked open my Jamaican soda drank it all in one sitting. Once I finished it, I picked up my plate and continued with my meal.

I finally finished my plate and was too lazy to even make it to my room, I kicked off my shoes right there and laid down on my couch and sleep instantly caught me.

"Ali help me, why won't you help me," I heard my girl Ashanti yelling out for me.

"I'm coming bae, just hold on," I replied running down the long hallway trying to get to her.

I finally walked into a semi dark room where Ashanti was sitting in a chair tied up in only her bra and panties in the middle of the room and this nigga Matrix was standing behind her with a gun in his hand wrapped around her shoulder.

"It's nice of you to join us my friend," He spoke with a smile on his face.

"Let her fuckin' go NOW," I yelled.

"Now why would I do that Ali huh? All it takes is one time, we've been waiting and watching. You never let her be alone, I told my guys just be patient it will happen and look I was right," He boasted.

"If you want me you got me, I'm here. TAKE ME INSTEAD OF HER," I challenged.

"Now what fun would that be if I did that?" He teased.

"Matrix I'm here and I'm alone if you want to kill me now you can, but I need for you to let her go," I spoke through clenched teeth.

I looked at Ashanti's beautiful face and she was so scared and it's all my fault, I promised her that my street life would never touch her and I failed her, now I had to get her out of here.

"Baby look at me, just stay calm, I'm going to get you out of here," I assured her.

"How are you making such promises to this lovely young lady?" He asked removing some hair from her face with the gun.

"You motherfucker," I yelled and started to go towards him.

He picked up the gun and pointed it at me.

"Don't you move motherfucker or I will kill you right now," He threatened.

I stopped right there in my tracks, I didn't want to do anything to anger him more. I was biting the inside of my mouth so hard I was tasting blood.

"Now we are going to play a little game, you like games right Ali?" He questioned.

"If I play your little game will you let her go?" I asked.

"That's only up to you my dear friend," He stated.

I took a deep breath and stood there and thought about my options, there wasn't a way I could get her out of here without playing this game. I didn't know where the hell Cobain was at, I sent him the location so he should be on his way, but time was running out.

"Are we playing or not Ali?" He asked again.

"Yea," I replied looking him in the eyes.

"Well my friend this is my favorite gun, real old school but it shoots great, it's a six-round shooter, but I only put three bullets inside. So, every time you get a question wrong I'll pull the trigger on your little girlfriend here" He told me.

"Nah I'm not about to play Russian roulette with my girl's life," I stated.

"Well it looks like you don't have much of a choice in the matter here huh since I'm the one holding the gun," He said in a matter of fact tone.

I looked around as the lights got a little brighter and saw that we weren't alone he had an army surrounding him and they were all holding guns. I was right now in a fucked-up predicament I could only hope Cobain gets here like now.

"Ashanti baby, I love you, and I'm going to get you out of here," I promised her.

I didn't know if it was true or not but I had to believe it, I loved this girl more than I loved myself and would do anything to see her smile right now.

"I... I love you too Ali," She whimpered.

"First question, what made you think you could kill my son and no have me retaliate?" He asked.

"Man fuck your pussy ass son," I yelled out.

"CLICK"

"AHHHHHHH" She screamed tugging at my heartstrings.

I heard as he pulled the trigger while the gun was at her temple.

"Fuck okay, shit. your son stole from us and tried to start his own business with our product. We didn't even know he was your son but even so you know the rules to the game," I shrugged.

"Question two- "

"Man, you a bitch ass nigga, why don't you let my shorty go. Rules are no women and children, and right now you violating all the rules fuckboy. You know this won't end good for you," I stated.

"CLICK"

"AHHHHHHHH OH MY GOD, PLEASE LET ME GO," She yelled out with tears cascading down her face.

"You still want to talk shit?" He taunted.

"NO," I barked.

"Now, where was I? Oh yes question two, even when you found out he was my son and you and your sidekick killed him, you don't think you owed me any explanation?" He questioned.

"An explanation for what? You know how the game goes, we learned from watching you growing up. If this wasn't your son this conversation wouldn't even be going on right now and you know that," I stated truthfully.

"Well he was my son, my ONLY SON, and y'all took him from me! So, it's only right I make you feel how I do at this moment," He spoke.

"CLICK,"

"Please… please… please…" I kept hearing Ashanti mumbling over and over.

"She's like a cat over here with all these lives she keeps getting," He laughed.

It was taking everything in me not to run up over there and put two in his dome but all these guns around me were making shit difficult for me to do anything.

"When I get my hands on you. You are going to regret that shit! I'm about to murder you like I did your bitch ass son," I threatened.

"BOOM"

"NOOOOOOOOOOOOOOOO ASHANTI," I YELLED.

I jumped up off the couch dripping sweat, my whole body was drenched. I put my hands over my face and just screamed into my hands. These nightmares were really starting to become more consistent and aggravating, I don't want to keep remembering how I failed her. It's been three years since she's been gone and it still feels like yesterday that I lost her. I walked upstairs to my room and went straight into the bathroom and cut the shower on and stepped out of my clothes and stepped into the water.

I stood under the water hose and just let the water run down my body, these jets were doing wonders to my body right now and I needed it. I need to figure out how to get these dreams under control, shit wasn't healthy at all. It was about to make me pick up a blunt again and that was something I wasn't trying to do.

I washed up quickly and got out the shower, I wrapped the towel around my waist then wiped the steam from off the mirror and looked at myself. I looked like a nigga was in need of a vacation shit was all fucked up right now and I just knew that this was just the beginning.

I walked out the bathroom and sat on my bed, a nigga was tired as fuck but I knew sleep wasn't coming to me no time soon, so I just decided to get dressed and take my ass to the hospital and check on my brother. I stood up and went to my dresser and grabbed a pair of Polo boxers and sprayed myself with some Tom Ford cologne and then went in my closet and found something to wear for the day.

***

I was sitting in the hospital room just looking at my man, he was here but not really here, and this shit is killing me right now. I feel like this is all my fault, I should have covered him better than I did.

"Hi, I'm Dr. Drake I'm the attending doctor that's overlooking Mr. Wade's case," The doctor walked in introducing himself and bringing me from my thoughts.

"Hey doc I'm Ali, Cobain's brother," I responded.

"Nice to meet you," He replied shaking my hand.

"How's he doing?" I asked jumping right into it.

"He's progressing, but it's up to him at this point. We did everything we could to help him. Now he just needs to wake up, his body is just tired because it worked harder than it had to when he got shot so basically, we just must wait," He explained.

"So, you're telling me that he could wake up today or months from now?" I asked for confirmation.

"That's exactly what I'm saying, all his vitals are good and the blood transfusion went well so now we just wait until he's ready," He explained.

"Okay, thanks doc," I responded.

"If you have any questions, please don't hesitate to ask," He replied before walking out.

"Bro, I'm going to need for you to wake the fuck up, you know I'm not good with shit like this, seeing you like this is making me feel like shit," I admitted.

I looked at him just wishing he would respond to me right now and tell me stop being a pussy with all this sweet talk.

"I got most of those niggas bro but that nigga Dragon got away, and I'm not comfortable leaving you here alone. You know I have niggas guarding you and shit but I don't know if any of these doctors are compromised,"

I sat there scrolling on my phone when I had the brightest idea, I hopped up and went to the nurse's station.

"Hey, I need to speak to a doctor but I don't know her last name," I said to the nurse that was sitting there.

She was sitting there giving me all kinds of googly eyes and shit, but the kicker is the bitch was low key cocked eyed. So, I really don't know if she was really giving me googly eye or she was just giving her regular look.

"Okay, no problem. What's her name?" She asked.

"Um all I know is Keri," I told her.

"Oh, that's doctor Keri Alexander, great doctor. Let me see if she's in for you," She said looking up at her charts.

"Thank you, I really appreciate it beautiful," I said causing her to blush.

She looked at me and now I knew for sure she was giving me googly eyes and the shit was giving me the creeps. Her eyes looked like that nigga from that movie Scary Movie, and she thought it was cute. I wanted to tell her stop making them things Crip walk like that.

"Her shift starts soon so as soon as she gets in would you like me to tell her to come see you?" She asked smiling at me.

"Yes please, I'm in room 406," I told her.

"No problem, as soon as she gets in I'll have her come see you," She assured me.

I walked away and went back into the room, I know if I can get her to help me I would feel a lot better with leaving him here. I sat back down and continued to talk to him as if he was here, I remember learning in school that even though they were in coma's they could hear everything around them.

Niggas wouldn't even know I went to school let alone graduated and have a college degree. My dad didn't play about school, he said he couldn't control what I did in these streets but if I lived under his roof school was a priority. So, I did one better not only did I graduate high school I also graduated with my bachelor's degree in business management. I might have been a street nigga but I was an educated street nigga and we were the most dangerous kind of niggas.

"Hello," I heard someone say in the softest voice.

I looked up and I saw Ms. Keri in her doctor gear, I had to admit it she was a sexy mother fucker and she was clearly on her shit which was always a good thing for a black woman.

"Hey Dr. Keri, thanks for coming," I acknowledged.

"Keri is fine, and no problem. What can I do for you?" She asked.

"First, I just want to say thank you for saving my brother and I'm sure when he wakes up he will be thanking you a million times also," I told her truthfully.

"Trust me it's no issue, I was just doing my job. I'm glad that I could help," She stated in a sincere tone.

"Can I trust you?" I asked looking her straight in the eyes.

"Umm, yes of course why would you ask me that?" She asked confused tone.

"I need a favor from you, and I'll pay you if need be," I told her straight up.

"I don't need your payment, and if I'm able to help you I will, now what do you need and be honest?" She asked.

I sat there and thought about what she was asking but I already knew I couldn't tell her the whole truth so I decided to just tell her enough to get her off my case.

"Listen you saved his life and honestly I don't want another doctor around him, so I need for you to get familiar with his charts because I only want you reporting to me with anything pertaining to his wellbeing," I stated.

She stood there and looked at me like I was crazy, I wasn't sure what she was thinking but she really didn't have a choice in the matter. I wasn't leaving here until she agreed to be his doctor.

"I have other patients and Dr. Drake is an amazing doctor I can assure you, he's in the best hands he can be in," She tried to persuade me.

"I don't think you heard me clearly, I want you and only you to be his doctor, and I'm not taking no for an answer," I told her honestly.

"Fine," She reluctantly agreed.

"Thank you, when I'm not up here I don't want him to have any visitors unless I clear them first. Can you make that happen for me?" I asked.

"I can let security know," She replied.

"Great, and as stated before you will be paid for your services," I repeated.

"Keep your money, it's my job and I took an oath. So, I will be his doctor," She assured me.

I sat there and spoke to her more on his condition and she pretty much told me the same thing the other doctor was telling me earlier. It was up to him to wake up when and only when he was ready. As soon as she walked out the door, a lightbulb went off in my head. I jumped out my seat and ran to the door to catch her.

"Hey doc," I called out.

She turned and looked at me then walked back to the room.

"Yes?" She responded.

"Put your number in my phone, since you never texted me," I told her handing her my phone.

She didn't immediately grab the phone which was kind of weird to me but I didn't dwell on it.

"I'll only text you if it pertains to my brother, I see that big rock on your finger and I'm not trying to step on any toes, I just want to be able to reach you without having to call the hospital for updates" I told her.

She once again reluctantly took my phone and put her number in it, then handed it back to me.

"Thank you," I said again.

"You're welcome," She replied and walked out the door.

I went and sat back down in my chair and started talking to my brother again, I hope all this talking is helping to bring this nigga back from the dead. We didn't even talk this much when he was awake.

Chapter 4- Cree

I was currently dancing to *DJ Khalid's Wild Thoughts* in my room getting ready for my date with this guy I met a few weeks ago in the supermarket. We've been texting consistently since we first met and he seems like a decent guy, but they usually all do in the beginning. While my face was setting I was in my closet looking for something to wear.

I pulled out a few different selections and placed them on my bed to see how I really felt about them. The weather was still kind of funny, it be nice now then drastically drop when you blink. I stood there and looked at each item before finally deciding on this wine-colored form fitting knee length dress and my black Christian Louboutin's.

I slid the dress on feet first so I wouldn't mess up my hair and makeup and slid the zipper up the side. I then slid my feet into my shoes and looked at myself in the mirror and had to admit, I was thoroughly impressed at what I was seeing, I was looking like a snack and couldn't wait for Koji to see me. I finished up my final touches on my face and switched purses and was ready to go.

    I decided to meet him there at the restaurant in case he turned out to be crazy, I didn't need him knowing where I lived at. I got in my car and plugged the Aux cord into my phone and blared *Miegos Slippery* through the speakers and pulled off to my destination. I drove the whole way there with that song on repeat to get me in the mood for my night.

    I pulled up to the restaurant and parked valet, I walked into the restaurant and looked around for Koji until I spotted him. I walked over to him and he was looking like a million bucks, he stood up and greeted me then pulled me in for a hug and he smelled so dam good, he made my knees buckle.

    "You are even more beautiful then I last remembered," He complimented.

    "Thank you," I replied blushing.

He walked to the side of me and pulled my chair for me to sit down after I caught him checking my ass out.

"Why thank you," I spoke.

"No thanks needed beautiful," He replied.

I picked up the menu and looked it over, I already knew what I wanted because I googled this place when he told me where I was going, but I had to play my part.

"How was your day?" He asked sipping on his water.

"It was okay, work was a drag though," I told him.

"What is it that you do again?" He inquired.

"I'm an interior decorator and the couple I was working with couldn't agree on shit, which made the day drag. It took hours to finally agree on a color for their bedroom, so that's how my day went," I told him.

"Sounds very interesting," He chuckled.

"Oh, it was," I replied laughing.

The waiter came over and took our drink order as well as our food order, then took our menus and walked off leaving us there alone again.

"So, tell me a little more about yourself," He probed.

"Um well let's see, well you know I'm 32. I'm an only child. My parents are still happily married, I love what I do for a living, I plan to be the next big thing around here soon. hopefully open up my own agency and be my own boss," I honestly spoke.

"Wow to hear you speak of this dream and to see the fire and desire in your eyes is simply amazing, I know that you really want this. I can't wait to see you accomplish all of this," He told me with the sincerest look on his face.

The waiter came back and placed our food I front of us, we both bowed our heads and said grace before digging in.

"So, tell me about yourself," I spoke before placing some food in my mouth.

"Well you already know I'm a law clerk, I still stay at home with my parents while I'm saving up for my own house. I have 4 kids, - "

"What?" I replied coughing.

I kept coughing as if I was choking, I picked up my glass of water and took a few gulps to try and help control my coughing.

"Why didn't you mention you had kids?" I asked finally able to catch my breath.

"Is that going to be a problem?" He questioned with the raise of an eyebrow.

"No of course not, I was just wondering why you didn't mention them," I replied.

"Well to be honest women usually run off when I tell them how many kids I have, and I was feeling you and didn't want to scare you," He stated.

I instantly felt like shit for wanting to jump out the bathroom window just now. It's not that I didn't like kids because I did, I just didn't want any EVER. Kids were cool but 4 was A LOT.

"I get it and I apologize if you felt that you couldn't tell me from the jump, its' fine. How old are your kids?" I inquired.

"Let's see Janiyah is 12, Jaqueal is 8, KJ is 3 and Americus is 8 months," He told me.

"8 MONTHS?" I asked in a low harsh tone.

"Yea is that a problem?" He asked like the shit he said was normal.

"Where is little Americus's mother?" I asked because this shit was getting out of control.

"She's at home where she's supposed to be taking care of my daughter," He stated as if I was supposed to know.

"So, you have an 8-month-old with her and you expect me to believe that you two are over?" I questioned.

"Actually, I do we haven't been together since we found out that she was pregnant with my daughter," He explained.

"Is she the mother to all your kids?" I quizzed hoping that he said yes.

"She the mother of my youngest two and the older two have a different mom. I was with her when I was in high school and we didn't work out but we are now great friends and co-parent very well together," He explained.

"That's... that's interesting to say the least," I admitted.

"I know it's a lot but I can promise you it's only a lot on paper, if we get further you will see for yourself beautiful," He spoke.

I just nodded my head and smiled as I sipped my wine, I don't know what the future held for us but right now it wasn't looking to bright. The night surprisingly did a 180, we ended up having an amazing time together. Besides finding out he had BeBe's kids I found out that we have a lot of other things in common. We discussed that our next date was going to be the museum of natural history and I couldn't wait for that, that was one of my favorite museums ever.

The night was coming to an end and he paid the bill then I excused myself to the bathroom before we left. I walked in the bathroom and went right in the stall, once I was done relieving my bladder I washed my hands then fixed my makeup in the mirror before I went back out to Koji.

"You ready to go beautiful?" He asked standing up as I walked back to the table.

"As ready as I'll ever be," I replied with a smile.

He placed his hand on the cusp of my back and guided me out the front door. Once we got to the front we both handed the valet our tickets and we waited for our cars to be brought around.

"Listen I'm not ready for the night to end just yet, I'm still having a good time with you," He spoke up.

"I'm actually having a good time with you also," I admitted.

"Great, so follow me back to my place?" He asked.

"I'm not really sure if that's going to be a good idea," I responded.

"It will be fine we can sit on my indoor porch and exchange more horror stories from our school days, I have some wine you can drink if you want if not I also have water," He said trying to persuade me.

I looked at him as he was giving me the puppy dog eyes and fake pout, then he brought his hands up as if he was begging and pleading for me to agree.

"Ugg fine Keith Sweat, I'll come but I can't stay long," I told him sternly.

"One hour tops beautiful," He smiled.

"Okay," I replied with a smile back.

Once valet pulled my car around he walked me to my car and helped me inside before shutting the door.

"Just follow me," He told me.

I nodded my head in agreeance with him and watched as he jogged back to his car and got inside. He pulled around me and beeped the horn then pulled off, I put my car in drive and pulled off behind him. I plugged my aux wire back into my phone and turned on that *Cardi B Bodak Yellow* new song and turned into a gangsteress on the way to his house.

He was trying to be on his fast and furious shit but the way my A8 was set up I wasn't too far behind and the only reason I didn't smoke him was because I didn't know where I was going. We pulled up to a nice ass house in a nice ass neighborhood, I parked in a spot right behind him and shut my car off and got out.

"This is nice," I complimented.

"Thanks, let's go" He said grabbing my hand and leading me up the stairs.

Once inside I saw that there were two doors, one to the left and one to the right. We went to the right, once he got that door open he hit the switch on the wall cutting the lights on and I was amazed at what I saw.

"Wow Koji your place is… nice and… clean for a bachelor pad," I commented.

"Thanks, I guess," He shrugged.

"Don't say it like that I'm just amazed that your place looks like this that's all," I admitted.

"No, it's cool I get it, men are usually messy" He smirked.

"What was that other door that we passed on the way in?" I asked.

"That was my parents side of the house and this is mine," He said taking off his shirt.

I stood there trying not to stare at him but dam it was hard as fuck, this man was sexy as fuck and I do mean sexy. He was giving any and everybody a run for their money right now and I wasn't even mad at him.

"You good ma?" He asked with a smirk showing off a little dimple on the left side of his cheek that I didn't even notice before.

He just got finer and finer every dam second.

"Yea fool, I'm good why wouldn't I be?" I asked as I squeezed my pussy muscles together.

"I was just making sure," He said winking at me.

Once he changed his shirt he grabbed my hand and led me out the room and down a hall, until we got to a porch.

He pulled up a chair and offered me a seat then cut on his fire pit.

"I'll be right back," He said.

He walked off the porch and I just looked around at my surroundings, his porch had an amazing view of the Brooklyn bridge that I fell in love with. I wouldn't mind seeing the sunrise from back here.

"I'm back," He announced.

He came back and had a bottle of wine and a glass along with a bottle of water just in case. He also had some Henny for him, he placed the stuff on the table then sat down next to me.

"This view is beautiful," I commented.

"Isn't it? I come out here when I need to think, it's just so peaceful and I get my best ideas for cases out here," He said.

"I can imagine," I replied.

I decided not to drink anymore so I reached for the bottle of water and opened it and took a sip from it. We both sat there in silence just enjoying the view, it was like a comfortable silence that I was actually enjoying.

"Cree?" I heard him call.

"Yes?" I responded.

"Can I kiss you?" He asked.

I felt his eyes on me but I never turned to face him, I wanted him to kiss me but the way that I was feeling I knew that it was a possibility that it could lead to more.

"Cree can I kiss you?" He asked again.

I nodded my head up and down and that was all he needed, he put his hand on my chin and turned my head to face him then slowly leaned into me and kissed me. This was the best kiss I've ever experienced in my life. It was soft yet rough, passionate yet controlled, it was just right.

"Dam," I whispered as I pulled away.

"Dam is right, I've wanted to kiss you since we were at the restaurant," He admitted.

He stood up and reached for my hand, I placed my hand in his and he helped me up then led me back inside.

Once we got back in his room, he couldn't keep his hands off me. He kissed my neck and collar bone as he lowered each strap on my dress. He unzipped the side of it and let the dress fall to the floor, I stepped out of it never missing a beat. He guided me to the bed and sat me down on it, he kept his eyes on me.

"Dam Cree you are so fuckin' sexy," He spoke.

He dropped his pants and boxers and I got a glimpse of that dick and I just knew I was about to get the shit fucked out of me, he then laid me on his bed and got on top of me, he started passionately kissing me again. He was making my pussy yet just from this so I couldn't wait to see what he did with his dick.

"Dam ma you wet as fuck already," He moaned.

He leaned over me and opened his draw and pulled a condom out, he used his teeth to open it and then he rolled it on his dick. He placed his dick on the entrance of my pussy causing me to gasp a little. He looked me in the eyes and slowly inserted his dick in me, I had to grab the sides of his shoulder as he slid in.

"Oh, fuck Cree, this pussy is tight," He said as he finally slid in.

He started pumping inside of me and as soon as it started to feel good and I was about to start fuckin him back it happened.

"Oh shit, ahhhhhhh. Fuckkkkkk Cree," He belted out.

I laid there not really sure if he was serious or not, but when he fell to the side of me and started snoring I just knew he was. I can't believe I fucked him and this is what I got, this man was to fine for his dick to be a waste.

I slowly and quietly got up and put my dress back on and picked up my shoes and tip toed out his house. When I got in my car I pulled my phone out and blocked his ass, there was no way in hell that I was ever seeing him again. I started my car and peeled off I couldn't wait to tell Keri about this shit right here.

Chapter 5- Keri

"Good Moring," Max greeted walking into the kitchen kissing me on the cheek.

"Morning," I replied with a forced smile.

I handed him his cup of coffee as he passed by to go get his paper, this has been our morning routine since I could remember.

"Is Khloe up for school?" He asked taking a sip of his coffee.

"Yup, I woke her when I got up, so she should be down here soon," I spoke as I poured myself a cup of coffee.

"I have an award banquet tomorrow that we have to be in attendance for, see if you can get your mom to keep Khloe," He told me.

"Okay Max," I responded.

"I want you to do your hair like I like it and wear that black Prada dress that you have in the closet that long one," He stated.

"No problem Max," I replied sipping my coffee.

"Good morning," Khloe greeted as she walked in the kitchen.

"Good morning, do you want breakfast?" I asked placing my cup on the table.

"Um no, just a cup of orange juice please," She said.

I got a glass out and poured her some, then handed her the glass.

"How are you feeling this morning Khloe?" Max asked her.

"Honestly, I feel good. I slept like a baby," She said with a smile on her face.

"That's good to hear," I spoke.

"You ready for school?" I questioned.

"Yup," She replied finishing up the rest of her orange juice.

"Perfect," I replied.

I grabbed my bag and kissed Max on the cheek and was about to walk out, but was stopped when he grabbed me by my elbow. He looked to make sure Khloe was out of sight before he spoke.

"Make sure you don't forget to check in dear," He said in a harsh whisper.

"I won't," I replied as best as I could since he was squeezing the hell out of me.

"Good, have a good day dear," He spoke then kissed me before he let me go.

"You too," I replied walking out the kitchen rubbing my elbow.

I got into my range rover and joined Khloe who was already in the backseat waiting for me. I stared the car and drove out the driveway en route to Khloe's school.

Khloe was my 16-year-old sister who I was taking care of since she almost died from an overdose two years ago because my mom wasn't watching her. My mom was one of those moms who had us young and thought because she got us to a certain part in life she didn't have to be a mom anymore. Unbeknown to me Khloe was left home alone plenty of times fending for herself while my mom was out and about being unfit.

I just happened to decide to stop by my mom house one day to take Khloe to the mall and found her passed out on the living room floor with a pill bottle next to her and I gave her CPR and saved her life. If I never showed up she would have died, and my mom acted like she didn't even care because she was so high her dam self.

So ever since then I sent my mom to rehab and Khloe came to live with Max and I, Khloe had to go to this rehab place that specialized in cases like Khloe's. I didn't realize how messed up and dependent on drugs she really was until she came to live with us. The rehab I placed her in she kept eloping and getting high again, so with the help of Max he was able to get her into one of the best rehab centers in the state. I made good money as a doctor but even my money wasn't enough to cover the bill for that.

    Today she was doing amazing she had minor slips here and there which I couldn't understand why when I gave her whatever she wanted, she was very spoiled by me. It was definitely a struggle at times but I would do it all over again for her. My mom was now clean but I still didn't trust Khloe to move back with her.

    If it wasn't for Khloe I wouldn't even be dealing with Max and his shit anymore, I couldn't afford her treatment on my own salary. I failed her once before and I wouldn't do it again, she was all I had in my life and I had to make sure she was good no matter what it did to me.

    "Khloe, you have money?" I asked looking in my rearview mirror.

    "Yea, I have a few dollars," She replied looking up from her phone.

    "Okay, good,"

We drove the rest of the way in silence and I was okay with that, I was trying to figure out how I could get out of this banquet with Max.

***

"So, spill it missy," I said staring at Cree.

I knew she had something to tell me by the way her ass was looking at me all stupid and shit.

"Come on girl my shift starts in fifteen minutes," I said looking at my watch.

We were currently in the hospital cafeteria catching up before I had to work but little miss Cree seemed to have lost her voice.

"You know what, when you're ready to talk call me, I'm not finna play with you today," I said getting up.

"Okay, okay, sorry," She laughed.

"I'm waiting," I told her.

"So, you know how I had my date with Koji last night right?" She quizzed.

"Yea I remember you telling me something like that, so what happened?" I asked.

She began telling me how perfect her night was and how he was a complete gentleman, and even after he told her he had four kids she still stayed and gave him a chance. For her to still stay after that revelation meant she was really feeling him because homegirl didn't do kids at all. Then she told me about the sex or lack thereof it.

"Wait what?" I asked in a confused tone.

"Yes, girl two pumps and a squiggle," She repeated then put her head down on the table.

I sat there in astonishment at what she just said, I just busted out laughing. I couldn't even help myself this shit was hilarious.

"People still fuck like that sis?" I asked through laughter.

"Apparently cuz that's how I got it last night," She groaned.

"So now what?" I inquired.

"Now nothing, I snuck out while his ass was snoring and blocked his ass, return to sender, do not pass go do not collect 200 dollars," Her dramatic ass said.

"Okay I get it," I laughed.

"It's not funny Keri, what's wrong with me why do I keep finding all the clown ass niggas?" She asked in a sad tone of voice.

"First off stop picking up guys off them stupid ass dating sites, - "I started to say.

"Well to help my case I met Koji in the supermarket," She interrupted.

"Just listen, stop looking for love. Let it find you when it's for you, you will know because all the right signs will be there. I can almost promise that your Mr. right isn't on tinder or Instagram," I joked.

"Yeah you right. Thanks for listening," She smiled and squeezed my hand.

"That's a part of the best friend contract," I joked.

"I guess I owe you ice cream for your services huh?" She asked.

"That's just the beginning," I replied sticking my tongue out.

"Whatever you need your royal highness," She said in the tone of that lady from the movie *Coming to America.*

"I like the sound of that, but I have to go now. Call me later," I told her standing up holing my arms out.

She moaned and groaned and stood up and walked into my arms and hugged me.

"Have a good day babe, I love you," I told her.

"I love you too sis," She replied.

We walked out the cafeteria arm in arm until it was time for us to part ways, she went out the revolving doors and I went to the elevator to my floor. I got off on the 4th floor and went to the nurse's station to check my assignments for the day. My first stop was to Mr. Wade, I went to my locker room and grabbed my coat and my badge putting it on. After I did that I went straight to Mr. Wade's room, I walked in and was greeted by the sounds of the machines. I walked up on him and checked his vitals.

"Good morning Mr. Wade I'm Dr. Keri, I'm here to check on you and make sure that everything is going accordingly," I spoke to him as if he was awake.

I looked at the monitor and his heartbeat and pulse were normal, I put my stethoscope in my ears and place the other end on his chest so I could hear how his lungs sounded.

"Well your lungs sound great," I told him.

I couldn't help but admire his handsome face, even though he needed a shave you could still see the beauty behind the beast. I wondered what could this man had done that was so bad that he deserved to be shot. I pulled his chart from behind the bed and marked down my observations for this hour then placed it back in the holder.

"I hope you wake up soon, your brother is pretty worried about you, I don't know you, but you look pretty tough. So, fight, fight to come back to us" I whispered in his ear.

I took one last look at him before walking out the room and heading back to the station.

"Hey nurse Carina can you get the physical therapist in room 406 please to move the patient's legs around so that they don't get stiff and he doesn't get bed sores please," I ordered.

"Yes Dr. Alexander," She responded.

"And please see that he gets wiped down, please," I added.

"No problem," She replied.

I continued with the rest of my rounds checking on my patient's. I felt my phone vibrate and pulled it out my jacket pocket and saw that it was a text message from Max.

Max: *wyd?*

Me: *makin' rounds*

Max: *what happened to you checkin' in?*

Shit I completely forgot after my talk with Cree, I knew he was about to pitch a fit.

Me: *sorry babe, as soon as I got to work I got dragged into the ER*

Max: *uh huh*

I dropped my phone in my pocket and continued with my rounds, I felt my phone vibrate and decided to ignore him, whatever he had to say was just going to have to wait until I got home later. After about an hour straight of checking in on people, giving out diagnosis and prescriptions I was in need of a quick break. I went and sat behind the nurse's station for to catch a breather.

"Today is crazy, it's like everyone got the memo to get hurt at the same dam time," The nurse joked.

"If I didn't see it for myself I wouldn't even believe you girl, and just think the day is just getting started," I stated rolling my eyes playfully.

When she was about to say something, I saw her eyes light up from behind me, I spun around in my chair to see what had her so hypnotized and that's when I saw Max walking off the elevator with a dozen red roses in hand and that signature smile on his face. Just that quick I thought back to the Max I first met all them years ago, he surely had me and the rest of the world fooled.

"Hey beautiful," He greeted handing me the roses.

"Hey, thank you for the flowers," I replied taking the roses from him and smelling them.

"Can your fiancé get some love?" He questioned.

"I'm at work babe," I said trying to play it off.

"Girl go hug your man, I won't tell anyone," The nurse responded smirking at me.

I put the flowers down on the desk and got up and walked around the desk and gave Max a hug.

"Let's go to a quiet room so we can talk," He whispered in my ear causing chills to run through my body.

"Hey, can you watch my post for a few minutes?" I turned and asked the nurse.

"Yeah of course girl, I got you take your time," She assured me with a smile on her face.

I led him down the hall away from everyone, so nobody would hear us. I found an empty room and led him inside of it. As soon as the door closed I instantly regretted leaving with him. He grabbed me by my arms and forced me against the door making me scream out a little.

"Shhhhhhh," He said with his finger against his mouth.

We stood there in silence for a minute, I guess to see if anyone heard me scream. When he saw that the coast was clear he began to speak.

"Why is it so hard to just do as I ask of you Keri? You used to always text me when you got to work and we use to text all the time," He said in a menacing tone.

His breath smelled like mints but you can tell he was just trying to cover up the liquor that he probably consumed after I left the house. Max was an oil tycoon and his business was booming since I've known him, but lately the company has been drowning in dept. and he's been drowning himself in alcohol and it's only been getting worse by the day.

"That's when you were different Max, you've changed over the years. This isn't the Max I know and fell in love with. The Max I fell in love with would never raise his hand to me," I stated looking him in the eyes.

He grabbed my face and squeezed it tight in his hands pushing my lips together bird like making sure he had a good grip before he decided to finally speak.

"Listen to me and listen good, things could get a lot worse before they get good again, don't fuck with me Keri. You wouldn't want that money for Khloe's school to just magically dry up now would you?" He threatened.

I shook my head no as the teas fell from my eyes.

"What's that I can't hear you, my sweet loving fiancé," He spoke in a whisper.

"No," I said as best I could.

"That a girl," He replied then kissing me on the lips before he finally let me go.

I stood there and stared at him with different ways that I could kill him and get away with it in my mind.

"Go clean yourself up," He said dismissing me.

I walked straight into the bathroom and looked at myself in the mirror to see if he left any bruises on my face. There wasn't anything yet but it was coming soon, I needed to get to my locker and get my makeup so I could cover up the bruises that were ready to make an appearance.

"Are we done here?" I asked.

He stood there looking me up and down and for the life of me I just couldn't figure out where we went wrong at. This man I was once head over heels in love is now the same man that I wouldn't spit on if his ass was on fire.

"Yes, get back to work. I'll see you when you get home later, and I want steak, potatoes and asparagus for dinner," He said walking up to me.

He leaned down and grabbed my face again then planted a kiss on my forehead.

"Have a good day baby," He spoke once he was done.

He turned and walked out the door just as fast as he came, and I couldn't be anymore happier. I sat on the bed and silently cried, I really didn't know how much more I could take of this. All I did know was that Khloe was depending on me and I couldn't let her down again. I wiped my tears and took a few deep breaths and prepared to make my way to my locker to fix my face.

I tried to take the back way to the locker room and ran smack dab into Cobain's friend Ali.

"Hey doc I was just looking for you," He said.

"Oh hey, I checked on Mr. Wade as soon as I came on shift and he's doing just great, if you have any questions I'll be happy to answer them as soon as I get back on shift," I told him trying to get around him.

He didn't even stop me which I was glad I was embarrassed enough and didn't want anyone to see my face before I had a chance to cover it up. I made it to the locker room and was thankful that I didn't run into anyone else on the way here. I opened my locker and pulled out my makeup bag then went and looked in the mirror. I had his finger prints on both sides of my cheeks, I applied a little concealer to the spots and when I felt like it was good I went back to my shift.

The rest of the shift went by pretty fast for the most part, I was there but wasn't really there. My mind wouldn't let me fully focus on what I needed to do, and as bad as I wanted to go home I'd rather stay here then go home and deal with Max and his shit. As a matter of fact, I was about to go see if I could pick up any overtime for the next couple of days.

***

I finally made it home after a 16-hour shift and tired was an understatement, I know Max was expecting me to cook but that wasn't happening tonight there was no way I would be able to cook.

"Finally, home I see," Max spoke starling me.

I looked up and saw him standing at the top of the steps with yet another glass of alcohol in his hand. I took a few deep breaths and mentally prepared myself for what could possibly go on tonight.

"Good evening baby," I greeted walking further into the house.

I placed my bag down on the table and walked into the kitchen to grab me a bottle of water before I hopped in the shower.

"Are you about to start dinner?" He asked walking in the kitchen behind me.

"Dinner now at this hour Max? I figured you would have eaten by now," I spoke feeling like some shit was about to go off.

"Yeah, I ate but it's not what I wanted, I waited for you to get home so you could cook my favorite. I even did a courtesy and took the meat out the freezer for you," He explained.

I looked in the sink and saw the pack of steak in the sink in a bowl of water waiting for me.

"Max I'm tired, I've had a long day can I just make you the steak tomorrow?" I asked in a pleading tone.

"So, because you're tired you expect me to starve dear?" He questioned in a you already know the answer to that tone?"

"Of course, not Max, let me take a shower and I'll get dinner started" I replied in a defeated tone.

I walked past him leaving him in the kitchen and walked up to the bedroom, I went in my closet and slowly took off my clothes and placed them in the hamper. I walked out the closet in only my panties and bra and was once again startled by Max sitting on the bed holding my phone.

"What are you doing with my phone?" I questioned.

"Who is Ali? And what is he thanking you for?" He asked ignoring my question and showing me my text thread.

"Ali is just one of my patient's brothers, and he's thanking me for checking on his brother. That's it nothing more nothing less," I explained.

"If that's the real situation why is he texting you personally and not calling the hospital for an update?" He asked getting up from the bed.

I slowly backed up until my back hit the wall, I looked at him not knowing what he was about to do.

"Don't be scared Keri I'm just asking you a question," He patronized.

"I'm telling you the truth Max, that's all it is. He just wanted to have contact with me since he requested me to personally be his doctor only," I told him.

"So, let me get this straight, out of allllllllll the doctors in that big ass hospital he personally chose you to be his brother's doctor?" He asked putting his hand on his chin.

"That's exactly right, why do I have to lie about that?" I quizzed.

"That's usually what people that are lying say," He responded with a shrug of the shoulders.

"Max I'm telling you that I'm not lying nothing is going on with me and that man," I pleaded for him to believe me.

"Okay, I believe you," He spoke.

I looked at him confused at what he just said this isn't like Max and I just know he has something up his sleeve.

"Go get washed up so you can make my dinner," He spoke before walking away.

I walked off and went straight to the bathroom and closed the door.

"KERI," He yelled.

I opened the door and s tuck my head out.

"Yes," I responded.

"If I find out that you're lying to me you will regret it, now hurry up in that bathroom," He threatened.

I didn't even bother to respond, I just closed the door and continued with what I was about to do. I was just grateful he didn't hit me this time, I turned the shower on and got in and prepared myself for this night that I was about to have.

Chapter 6- Cobain

One week later

I was laying in this bed hearing everything and everyone around me, I was trying to open my eyes but my body wouldn't cooperate with me no matter how hard I tired. I heard Ali here every day trying to coach me to wake up and it was frustrating because I just couldn't. I kept hearing that sexy doctor's voice in my ear also.

She was trying to get me to wake up but still nothing. I was coaching myself everyday but I still wasn't strong enough to wake up. If I could just give them a sign that I was here they wouldn't be so dam worried about me.

"Hi daddy," I heard from my princess then felt her kiss me.

I couldn't even respond to her this shit was killing me right now.

"Why isn't he waking up uncle Ali?" She questioned with a sad voice.

"He's still sleeping baby girl and his body has to heal and get stronger so he's able to wake up. But just keep talking to him, the doctor said he can hear us and it will help him wake up faster," He told her.

"Baby please wake up for us," I heard Shyne say with her dramatic ass.

I felt someone get on the bed next to me and grab my hand, I felt how little it was and that's when I figured out it was my baby girl.

"Daddy, please wake up. I miss you, and your hugs and kisses. You owe me a trip to the aquarium like you promised," She spoke sounding like she was on the verge of tears.

Wake the fuck up Cobain, get up now. Your daughter needs you. You never failed her before and you can't start now. I tried to force myself to wake up but nothing worked.

"Look mommy daddy is crying," Kaylee said wiping the tear that escaped from my eye with her hand.

I felt so helpless right now and there wasn't a thing I could do right now but lay here and hear my family cry out for me to wake up.

"Come on princess let's sit in the chair," Shyne told her.

"NOOOOOO, I want to stay here next to my daddy," She wined.

"It's cool, just leave her," Ali replied.

I felt her lie her head on my chest and she started singing our song that we sang to each other.

"No one loves me just like you do, no one knows me like you do,

No one can compare, to the way my eyes fit in yours,

You'll always be my father, and I'll always be your joy,

I tried to match your breathing, beating my little heart against yours,

Perfect were the nights, we were sleepin'

I never wanna end what we are" she sang so beautifully.

"That was amazing princess, I'm sure your daddy enjoyed hearing that from you," Ali told her.

"Do you think it would make him wake up faster?" She asked with a little cheer in her voice.

"It just might baby," Shyne answered.

They all sat around talking to me and each other for the next few hours, which I really enjoyed hearing. I was still trying to get my body to wake up so I could just hug my baby, I needed her to know that I was here for her.

"Okay baby girl, it's getting late and we need to get you home and ready for bed," Shyne spoke.

"Noooooo mommy I don't want to go, I don't want to leave daddy alone," Kaylee screamed and cried.

"Princess, I'll come get you tomorrow and bring your back up here myself," Ali said trying to get her to calm down.

"NOOOOOOOOOO, I don't want to go," She yelled.

"That's enough Kaylee," Shyne said in a stern voice.

"I just don't want to leave daddy here all alone," She whined.

"I know, but he's not alone he has a great doctor that checks on him all the time and makes sure he's good," Ali spoke.

"Are you sure he's going to be okay?" She asked.

"Have I ever lied to you baby girl?" He questioned.

"No," She replied.

"Exactly and I'm not going to start now," He assured her.

"Okay, bye daddy. I love you and I'll be here to see you tomorrow," She said then kissed me on the cheek.

I felt her get down off the bed then grab my hand and rubbed it. Eventually her hand left off mine and then they were gone. I laid there fighting my own body to regain control of my body. I heard the door open again and I heard a voice coming closer to me and my heartbeat began to increase a little.

"Why the sudden increase Mr. wade?" I heard her ask.

When I assumed it was a nurse my heartbeat slowed back down, she checked my vitals and just when I thought she was done I felt her hand on my dick.

"Dam Mr. Wade not only are you fine but you are packing, even on soft you are definitely not to be touched," She said as she gripped my dick harder.

When she started caressing my dick more getting it harder she got paged to another room.

"I'll be back," She whispered then walked out.

Open your fuckin' eyes now, you can do it. Push through and wake the fuck up. I fought with myself for what felt forever. Then next thing I know my eyes opened and it took me a while to get adjusted to the lights again but that was something minor to a giant. The hard part was over.

***

"Good morning Mr. Wade," I heard a familiar voice say.

"Good morning doctor," I replied.

She looked up from her note pad and looked at me with a shocked expression on her face.

"When… when did you wake up?" She questioned walking over to me and turning off the machine.

"Last night," I replied taking her all in.

"You gave us all quite a scare," She spoke as she put the stethoscope on my chest.

I looked her up and took in all her beauty, she was so fuckin' beautiful and a doctor shorty was on her game.

"Deep breath please," She instructed.

I took a deep breath in and released it.

"Again please," She asked moving to my back.

I did as she asked and waited for her to finish her job before I spoke to her.

"Thank you, well it looks like everything is good with you, I want to order some more test for you and if they come out good we can discharge you in a few days," She explained.

"Cool, how long have I been out?" I questioned.

"About a week," She responded.

"Dam that long huh?" I said rubbing my face.

"Yup, do you need anything or would you like me to call your brother?" She asked.

"As a matter of fact, yea tell him to get his ass up here," I stated.

"I can do that for you," She replied laughing.

"Thank you, excuse my appearance I usually don't look like this. It's been a long week," I joked.

"It's totally fine," She smiled showing the most perfect set of teeth.

"Is there any way that I could get some water?" I asked.

"Yes of course, I'll send someone to in here to get you whatever you need while I get in contact with your brother," She said turning to walk out.

"I heard you," I announced.

"Excuse me?" She stopped and turned with a confused look on her face.

"I heard you, when you spoke to me. Hell, I heard everyone but your voice was so… angelic and soft. I heard you telling me to fight and I appreciate that because you didn't have to," I stated truthfully.

"I was just doing my job," She replied with a smile and walked out.

I sat there happy as hell to finally be awake and to hear the voice that's been talking to me. I couldn't wait to see my baby girl and let her know I heard her singing our song. Soon as Ali brought his ass up here I was going to have him convince the doctor to let me go the fuck home today, fuck all that other shit she was talking shorty was fine as hell but not that dam fine to convince me to stay here any longer.

Chapter 7- Ali

"Well he was my son, my ONLY SON, and y'all took him from me! So, it's only right I make you feel how I do at this moment," He spoke.

"CLICK,"

"Please… please… please…" I kept hearing Ashanti mumbling over and over.

"She's like a cat over here with all these lives she keeps getting," He laughed.

It was taking everything in me not to run up over there and put two in his dome but all these guns around me were making shit difficult for me to do anything.

"When I get my hands on you. You are going to regret that shit! I'm about to murder you like I did your bitch ass son," I threatened.

"BOOM"

"NOOOOOOOOOOOOOOOOO ASHANTI," I yelled running over to her body that was now slumped over in the chair.

Just at that same moment Cobain and the crew came in guns blazing but I couldn't move I untied her and just held her in my arms.

"I'm so sorry baby,"

My phone ringing caused me to jump up from my dream, which I was thankful for, I reached for it but missed the call. I was drenched in sweat as usual. I saw it was the doctor so I quickly dialed her back as I made my way into the bathroom to cut the shower on.

"What's up doc is everything okay?" I questioned as soon as she picked up the phone.

"Yes, yes, I was just calling to let you know that he's awake now and he's asking for you to come see him now," She told me.

"Ight bet good looks doc I'll be there shortly," I replied hanging up the phone.

I tossed the phone on my bed then, then threw my wet clothes on the floor and hopped in the shower. I think I'm going to have to probably go see someone about this, this shit was starting to become a little more frequent now and I didn't understand why. I finished showering and dried off then went in my closet and looked for something to wear.

When I looked over at the calendar and saw the date that's when it hit me, it was coming up on the anniversary of Ashanti's death. That's why the dreams were becoming more frequent, I had to go by her grave and put some fresh flowers and talk to her make sure she's good. I grabbed some clothes off the hanger and picked up a pair of sneakers then walked out my closet.

I sat on the edge of my bed and ran my hands down my face, a nigga was beat and was in dire need of a vacation and some good sleep. I just knew that after this was all squared away I was going to be out for a few days. I went and put on some boxers and a T then threw my clothes on and made my way to the hospital to go see my brother.

***

"My nigga my nigga," I greeted with a smile on my face walking into the room.

"My nigga," He replied chuckling.

I walked further into the room and gave my man a hug, I was glad his ass finally woke up.

"How you feeling?" I asked after we released from the hug.

"I'm a little sore, but I'm good glad to be awake," He responded.

"Shit, you had us all worried about you, especially baby girl she was in here cuttin' up over your ass," I told him.

"I know man, I heard her." He said shaking his head.

"You heard her?" I asked confused.

"Yeah, I was awake but not awake if that makes sense, I could hear everything around me, but my body wouldn't allow me to wake up," He explained.

"Dam that crazy, not having control of your body like that," I said.

"Word but a nigga is back and ready to get up out of here," He said anxious.

"What the doctor saying?" I asked him.

"Some shit I aint really trying to hear right now, I've been in here long enough and either she gives me my discharge papers or I'm walking up out of here against her order," He stated in a matter of fact tone.

"I'll see what she's talking about but you need to listen to whatever she tells you, shorty really on her shit so I'm sure she not telling you nothing that's not good for you," I explained.

"I'm sure she's not but a nigga needs to get out of here, I'm trying to shower, shave and see my princess. I just don't have it in here to give her another few days," He stated.

"I hear you bro I'll give her a call," I said shaking my head.

"Appreciate it,"

"You know that doctor of yours, right?" I asked.

"Yeah what about her?" He asked staring at me.

"She's the reason your alive," I told him.

"What you mean?" He asked with a suspicious face.

I sat there and told him how she was the one that found him on the streets and saved his life. If her and her homegirl didn't walk that way that night you would have been dead bro.

"Dam, so not only did she find me she's my doctor also, huh" He said.

"Yeah when I found out she worked here I personally asked her to be your doctor, I don't know what kind of pull that nigga Dragon has and I wasn't going to leave you here with any of these nurses that could probably be bought," I spoke.

"My nigga, I appreciate that, speaking of nurses that's how I woke up," He admitted.

"What you mean that's how you woke up?" I asked looking at him.

"Check this shit out a fuckin' nurse came in here trying to jack me off getting my dick, all hard then got called away that's when my eyes opened," He said sounding like he was disgusted.

"Dam bro was it that bad?" I laughed

"Fuck up fool, when I hear her voice again I'm choking the fuck outta her ass," He said sounding pissed off making me laugh harder.

"It's nice to finally see some life in this room," We heard from the doorway.

We both stopped laughing and looked towards the door, and there was the doctor gracing us with her presence.

"Hey doc," I spoke.

"Good to see you again Ali," She greeted.

"How are you feeling Mr. Wade?" She asked focusing on him.

"I feel great actually, so I think you should let me go home today," He tried to convince her.

"As much as I don't want to see you in this bed anymore I need you to stay a little longer just so I can make sure your perfect," She explained.

"I get it doc maybe we work something out, because I'm really not trying to be here any longer," He told her.

"I'll see what I can do for you Mr. Wade," She said with a smile.

"Now my brother over here tells me that it's because of you I'm even still here, is that true?" He asked her.

"I was just doing my job," She replied.

"Look at her Ali being all modest and shit," He joked.

"I'm not at all being modest, it's the truth," She blushed.

"Well I just want to thank you for doing your job and saving me, I owe you, so if you need or want anything just let me know and I got you," He told her seriously.

"Thank you, but just as I told your brother I'm fine, thank you though," She again turned down.

"I'm not giving up on you yet, I owe you and I don't like owing people," He replied.

"I'll keep that in mind, I'm going to give y'all some privacy I'll be back before I leave. If you need anything you know the number," She said turning and walking out the room.

"Dam shorty is bad as fuck," He complimented looking over at me.

"Yeah, she is," I admitted.

We sat in the room chopping it up about our next moves and how we were going to handle Dragon once he was back at 100. It felt good to be talking my brother again, because just a week ago I didn't think I would be able to anymore.

"It's good to have you back bro," I told him truthfully.

"Man don't start that emotional shit, you were in here talking when I was knocked out," He joked.

"Man fuck you," I laughed.

"Nah I'm joking it feels to be back, and thanx for holding it down," He told me seriously.

"Man, you know that wasn't about shit. you know I got you," I said holding out my hand to him.

"As I do you," He replied as we did our handshake.

We finished talking and waiting for the doctor to come back and let us know if we were getting out of here today. I already knew if he had anything to do with it he was discharging today whether Dr. Alexander approved it or not.

Chapter 8- Cree

"Heyyy girl," I greeted Jazzy as I walked into the salon.

"Hey girl, just give me a few more minutes and I'll be done with her and your next," She replied curling the girl in her seats hair.

"Okay cool, no problem," I responded taking a seat in the waiting area.

I pulled out my phone and saw I had a text from an anonymous number but once I read the message I already knew who it was and I instantly caught an attitude.

"Girl who pissed in your cheerios because your face right now is extra stink," Jazzy spoke.

"Man, this nigga that I blocked long time ago just text me from this text free app begging me to unblock him," I said annoyed.

"Well what did he do for you to block him?" She quizzed.

I sat there and told her about our date and had the whole shop cracking up, this shit was embarrassing as fuck, but funny as hell now that I thought more about it.

"Girl he finessed the hell out of you," Jazzy joked.

"Girl did he, bad enough he had 4 dam kids and 2 baby mamas I still was willing to fuck with him only to be let all the way down," I stated getting mad all over again.

"Well better you found out now before you really started liking him," She pointed out.

"Yeah you right about that, I probably would have hit him with my dam car, then beat up his mama then fuck his daddy and make him my step son for fuckin' with my heart," I said laughing.

"You are crazy as hell girl, come on and get in this chair," She replied laughing.

"Hey, it's me I'm at Jazzy's salon can you drop me off some money please, I didn't realize I left my wallet home, I'm done now so I'll be here waiting. Thank you, love you," I heard the girl at the counter say into her phone.

    I watched as she sat down and waited for whoever she called to come drop her off some money. Jazzy took my added her secret hair crack in my head then took me to the back to wash it out. I was trying my hand at this natural thing but a bitch was missing her weave something so I said F my natural shit right now and I told her to slap some tracks in my head.

    After I got from under the sink I went straight to her chair so she could blow dry my hair instead of me sitting under the dryer. Soon as she started my hair in walked that dam Ali, I haven't seen him since that night in the hospital but he wasn't hard to forget. When he got further in him and I locked eyes and it's like time stood still for a quick second, but once I saw him walk over to ol girl and hand her some money that shit sped right the fuck on up.

    "Thank you, Ali," She spoke hugging him.

    "You know I got you," He replied.

She went and plaid then waited for him to follow her out but before he left he turned and winked at me before leaving out the salon.

"The nerve of that nigga," I stated shaking my head.

I continued talking to Jazzy as she slayed my hair for the gods, I ended up with a side swept bang and the rest long on my Aaliyah shit and I was feeling myself right now.

"Thank you, girl, you definitely hooked me up with this right here," I stated looking at my reflection in the mirror.

"Well you know I try," She joked patting herself on the back.

"You don't try you do and when you do we come out looking like this," I bragged.

I tipped Jazzy then went and paid bill then left. I stopped at Wendy's and grabbed me a salad and a strawberry lemonade then went straight to my house for a nap then I had to run to my office for a few hours.

***

I know I told Keri I was going to chill on dating and wait for my prince to find me but how can I find my prince if I don't kiss the frogs right? So right now, I had another date with this guy I met by my office. Nothing major just a little date at Cold Stone ice cream shop and hopefully good conversation, I threw on my distressed boyfriend jeans and a crop top and a pair of vans. I wanted to be comfortable in case we decided to go walking around anywhere.

Once I was fine with my outfit I put on a nude lip and was out the door. I got in my car and as usual hooked up my phone and blasted me some Jeezy, couldn't nobody tell me I wasn't in a trap house cooking up dope when I was listening to my trap music. Twenty minutes later I was pulling up to my destination, I parked my car and checked my lipstick one last time before getting out the car. I walked inside of the store and looked around for my date when I finally spotted him at a table in the middle of the store.

"Hi Deviin," I greeted walking up to the table.

"Hello, Cree. Dam you are even more beautiful dressed down," He complimented standing up.

He gave me a hug, it wasn't a prolonged hug which I appreciated.

"You want to get the ice cream now?" He asked.

"Sure," I replied.

We walked over to the counter and ordered our stuff, which he paid for and then we went and sat back at our table.

"I'm so glad you could make today to hang with me," He said before he stuck some ice cream in his mouth.

"Me too, I love ice cream and hopefully good company," I replied putting a gummy bear in my mouth.

We sat and had amazing conversation and realized we had a few things in common. Unlike the last guy he had no kids which I was grateful for and he also told me that he was a kindergarten teacher which I thought was pretty cool. By the time we finished our ice cream I found out a lot about him that made me like him a little more then I already did.

We left the ice cream place and walked down the strip just talking and laughing, I was really having a good time with him and wasn't looking forward to the night ending. I could really see myself dealing with him for the long run if it kept up.

"Hey, it's getting pretty late and I really don't want to say goodbye yet, so what do you think about coming back to my place. we can order Chinese and watch some movies," He suggested.

I stood there contemplating if I really wanted to go or not, I wasn't trying to mess up a perfect date by having a fucked-up night.

"I see the look on your face I promise you that I won't try nothing with you, I'm just not ready to let you go yet," He spoke trying to persuade me.

Against my better judgement I reluctantly agreed to go to his house to finish our date. We walked back towards the ice cream shop and I led him to my car and he got inside with me as I drove him to where he parked his car, once I dropped him there I waited for him to get inside then I followed him to his house.

  He lived about thirty minutes from where we met, the drive was relatively quick though. Pulling up to his house I was amazed at how big it was, I shut the car off and opened my door as Deviin was walking over to me. he grabbed my hand and led to his door.

  "Your house is beautiful," I told him as he opened the door.

  "Thanks," He replied closing the door behind me.

  Once he cut the lights on I was in complete awe of this man's house, it looked like something that I see on HGTV. The further we walked the more in love I was, once we got to his bedroom I completely lost it, his room was bigger than my whole dam apartment.

  "Let me get the menus so we can order, make yourself at home," He told me walking out the room.

  "Okay," I replied.

I walked around his room looking at all his high school trophies and awards, he was definitely a jock in school. I took my sneakers off and sat on his bed and turned the television on looking for something to watch.

"I see you made yourself comfortable already," He chuckled walking back in the room.

"Yeah, I hope that's okay?" I asked with a pout.

"Yeah, it's fine," He said closing his door and handing me the menu.

Once I figured out what I was going to eat he put the order in and we found a movie to watch on Netflix. The food finally arrived and before we dug in he requested that we say grace which caught me by surprise but I wasn't mad at him. After he said grace we dug into our food and continued with our movie.

After about the third movie we were barely hanging on, we were both dosing off and on so I decided to finally call it a night.

"Hey Deviin, I'm going to head in home it's getting late," I told him shaking him to wake him up.

"Hmm, no don't go its fine stay. I don't want you driving this late alone anyway," He replied in a groggy voice.

I really didn't wanna leave anyway because I was barely making it now as is. So, I said fuck it and got in the bed with him and was instantly knocked right out. I felt him come up behind me and wrap his arm around me and just that fast he was out again.

"DEVIIN," I heard a female voice call out making me jump up out my sleep.

I just know this nigga wasn't living with a bitch, and got me laid up in here with his ass.

"Deviin someone is calling you," I said shaking him causing him to pop up.

"What… what happened?" He asked rubbing his eyes.

"There's some woman calling your name," I told him in an annoyed voice.

"OH SHIT, STAY HERE, PLEASE," He said jumping out the bed.

I watched as he ran out the room closing the door behind him, that's when I got out his bed and through my shoes on. I was ready for whoever the fuck that was calling his name. After a few minutes, he came back in the room with a look on his face that I couldn't read.

"WHO THE HELL IS THAT DEVIIN" I yelled.

"Man keep your voice down," He spoke running over to me trying to quiet me.

"Don't tell me to be quiet, who the fuck is that?" I asked again.

"That's my mom and she can't know you're up here, I'm not allowed to have company stay over," He had the nerve to admit to me.

I stood there looking at him like he done lost his dam mind, we were two grown ass adults and I was not about to be hiding out in the man bedroom like a got dam teenager.

"You have got to be kidding me right now Deviin," I asked in an astonished tone.

"I know I'm sorry, I wasn't expecting her to be home so early," He admitted.

"You are a grown man and you're sitting here telling me that you aren't allowed to have company in your room. I can't believe this shit right now," I spoke.

"I know and again I'm sorry, can you just keep your voice down please. I'm going to go downstairs and talk to her and try to get her out the house then I'll text you and you can sneak out the house and leave," He had the nerve to say to me.

I stared him down and if looks could kill he would have been dead 10xs already, when I leave out of here I swear I was taking Keri's advice and just going to wait for my knight in shining armor to find me because this shit was getting out of hand now, I just couldn't catch a break.

"I swear I'll make it up to you," He said looking at me.

"Oh, you don't have to worry about making it up to me, because once I leave here you won't hear from me again. Better I tell you now then you find out when your blocked," I stated in a matter of fact tone.

He looked at me like he wanted to protest what I was saying but I didn't give a fuck, he had me all the way fucked up. He shook his head and walked out his room and closed the door behind me I stood there pacing back and forth pissed off that I even agreed to this shit. I grabbed my purse and walked out his room and down the steps where I saw him in conversation with a lady that I was assuming was his mom but she didn't look anything like him.

"Who…. Who is this Deviin?" His mom asked staring at me.

The look on his face was priceless and he didn't even know what to say or how to reply to her and this shit was sad as fuck.

"This is my friend mama," He replied staring at me.

"Deviin, is she a negro?" She had the nerve to ask me.

"MAMA," He yelled.

"You are lucky that I'm saved or I would be reading your racist ass mother for filth," I stated then walked out the house slamming the door behind me.

"CREE, wait up I'm sorry for that," I heard him call from behind me.

"I don't have anything to say to you Deviin so, I think it would be in your best interest to just leave me the hell alone," I demanded getting into my car.

I quickly stared it up and pulled the hell off leaving him standing there right in the middle of the street. My phone started ringing and picked it up and saw it was him calling me, I sent him to voicemail. It immediately rang again so I answered it.

"Cree, just wait let me explain," He yelled through the phone.

"Stop calling my phone before I have your house shot the fuck up, don't let the bougie fool you I'm still a hood bitch. Now if you know what's good for you let this be the last time you ring my phone," I threatened before hanging up on him.

I tossed the phone in the passenger and drove straight to my house so I could soak in the tub and drink off a bottle of wine.

Chapter 9- Keri

"Mom you home?" I called out walking into her house with Khloe following behind me.

We walked closer inside and found her in the living room watching her stories smoking a cigarette.

"Hey ma, you didn't hear me calling for you?" I asked standing in the doorway looking at her.

"Yeah, but my stories are on and you know how I hate being interrupted," She stated never taking her eyes off the TV.

"I hear you," I replied shaking my head and walking into her kitchen.

Khloe went to the backyard and sat on her pool ledge and stuck her feet in the water as she usually does whenever we come over here. I went in the fridge and grabbed a bottle of water and sat ay her island scrolling through my social media until my mom stories were over. Twenty minutes later

I heard her coughing and it sounded like she was coughing up a lung so I decided to take her a bottle of water.

"Here," I said handing her the bottle.

"Thanks," She replied opening it and drinking from it.

When she was done she placed it on the table and lit another cigarette, all I could do was shake my head at her. She literally went through a pack a day now since she wasn't getting high anymore.

"What brings you by?" She asked looking over at me.

"I just wanted to talk to you," I admitted.

"YOU? The infamous Dr. Keri Alexander, what can little ol me do for you?" She sassed.

"Mom don't do that," I told her.

"Do what? I'm just speaking the truth. I know u haven't been the best mom to you and your sister but I did my best and I'm proud of that and I'm proud how you turned out," She spoke sincerely.

I put my head down and just took in what she said, she wasn't the best but she wasn't the worst either but when it all came down to it I only have one mother so I dealt with it and loved her as best I could.

"Now what can I do for you?" She asked before taking a pull of her cigarette.

"Mom I don't know what to do with Max anymore," I spoke.

"What you mean baby? What are you trying to do with him?" She asked.

I took a deep breath and thought about my next statement and how I was going to tell her that he isn't the Max she met all them years ago.

"Come on baby spit it out," She spoke.

"Mom he… he hits me," I finally admitted to anyone for the first time in life.

"Hit you?" She asked in a shocked tone.

"Yes mom, he hits me. It's like as soon as I agreed to be his wife he changed and he started hitting me, and I don't know how much more of this I can take," I spoke on the verge of tears.

"Well Keri what do you be doing for that man to hit you baby?" She had the audacity to ask me.

"Are you fuckin' serious right now?" I yelled standing up.

"I know you better calm your ass the hell down, I'm still your mother and you're going to respect me as such," She stated.

"You want me to respect you as my mother when I just told you that this man is putting his hands on me and your response is what am I doing to make him hit me?" I shouted.

She pulled out another cigarette and lit it and took a pull before releasing it and speaking.

"That man isn't just hitting you for no reason, that's all I'm saying," She explained.

"Mommy he shouldn't be hitting me at all, what is wrong with you?" I asked through tears, that I couldn't hold back anymore.

"Listen to me Keri you have made a wonderful career choice for yourself but when it all boils down to it, with the money you are making you still can't afford to house me and pay for Khloe's school and rehab without Max. So, the truth of the matter is we can't lose him, so whatever it is you're doing just… just stop Keri before you fuck it up for all of us," She said seriously.

I just sat there with tears coming down my face listening to my own mother basically tell me that I needed to continue to let this man hit me.

"Keri… I know this isn't what you expected me to say, but it's the truth. Whatever he asks of you just do it and don't piss him off. It really isn't that bad, your dad used to knock me around a few times back in the day. You get used to it after a while," She shrugged taking another pull of her cigarette.

"I have to go mom, can you just keep Khloe for a little while I need to run a few errands and I'll be back for her in a little while," I said walking towards the door.

"Yeah, sure I got her," She replied.

I walked out the door and got in my car and I felt myself having an anxiety attack, I took a few deep breaths and tried to control my breathing. I turned my car on and put the air conditioning on high to help with my breathing. Once I felt like I was calm I put the car in park and drove off with no destination in mind. After about ten minutes of driving in a circle I decided to go to the mall and just walk around and clear my head maybe pick something up for myself or Khloe.

Pulling up into the mall, I parked my car and headed into the mall. I wasn't really in the shopping mood but being out and about was what I was needing right now with the way I was feeling. I felt my phone vibrate and I saw that it was Cree calling but I wasn't in the mood to talk to her now so I ignored her call, I would just call her back later when I got home.

I walked aimlessly around the mall going from store to store looking at stuff I knew I really wasn't the least bit interested in. I ended up in the food just sitting there by myself lost in my thoughts until I heard a voice behind me.

"Wassup doc," I heard then turned to look behind me and smiled when I saw who it was.

"Hello, Mr. Wade, I see you still left after I said not to" I said with a sarcastic tone and a smile.

"Well you know doc I had stuff to do and couldn't be cooped up in a hospital bed any longer," He admitted.

"I guess I understand," I told him.

"What you doing here?' He questioned.

"Nothing really just came to clear my mind," I replied.

"So, you came to the mall to do that? No offense doc but the mall isn't the right place to come to clear your mind," He stated.

"I'm starting to see that now and please call me Keri," I chuckled.

"Well Keri, do you mind if I join you or are you waiting for someone?" He asked.

"Where are my manners I'm sorry, yes please have a seat," I told him.

I watched as he put his bags down then pulled the chair out and sat down, his whole aura sang confident and he just knew he was the man. It was just something mysterious about this man that sat in front of me.

"So, what's on your mind? Maybe I can help you get over it, I use to be a therapist in my past life," He joked.

"Trust me even Dr. Phil?" can't help me with my problems," I stated with a light grin.

"Try me," He stated seriously.

I sat there looking him in the eyes and almost for a second thought about telling him about my problems but that thought quickly went away.

"No, it's fine, I'll be fine. What did you get from the mall bag man," I joked changing the subject.

"I see what you're trying to do and I'm going to let you for now, but we will get back to why you're in the mall looking all sad and shit. Every time I've ever saw you, you always had a smile on your face so to see you now like this is really fuckin' with me," He stated looking me in the eyes.

"I'm fine," I replied.

"You're not but it's cool, I'll play your game. I came to pick me and my daughter up a few things," He said shocking me.

"You have a daughter, that's nice. How old is she?" I asked.

"Yeah, her name is Kaylee and she's six, going on sixteen but that's my princess and I wouldn't have it any other way," He replied with a grin as his eyes lit up.

He then pulled out his phone and showed me a picture of his daughter and I immediately fell in love with her. She was so freakin' beautiful and she looked just like him. I couldn't wait to have my own kid but as long as I was with Max I wouldn't have one, there was no way in hell I was giving him a baby.

"She's so pretty, god bless you," I told him.

"Thank you, Ms. lady, do you have any kids?" He inquired.

"No, I don't," I replied.

"Shocking you look like you would be a great mom," He stated.

"Thanks, I'm actually taking care of my sixteen-year-old sister and she's giving me a run for my money already," I laughed.

"I can only imagine, teenagers these days are different," He spoke.

"Tell me about it," I said as I checked the time on my watch.

"Do you have to be somewhere?" He asked me.

"No not really," I replied.

"Okay good then come with me," He said grabbing my hands and his bags and leading me out the mall without giving me a chance to say anything.

I followed behind him and allowed him to lead me out the mall and to his car, once we got there I watched as he put his bags in the car and opened the passenger door for me. When I didn't immediately jump in the car he gave a weird look.

"Get in the car doc," He spoke.

"Where are we going?" I asked hesitantly.

"For a drive now get it," He stated.

I stood there and just looked at him not sure if I should even be entertaining him right now, but what was the worst that could happen so I through caution in the wind and got in the car with him. Once he closed the door that's when I started thinking crazy thoughts, I rarely even knew this man and he just got shot what if the person that shot him is still after him and decides to shoot the car up with me inside. When he got in I turned and looked at him.

"I don't think this is a good idea," I told him.

"Doc I got you trust me, whatever you're thinking stop. Your good," He stated in a sincere tone and something about the way he said it made me believe him so I sat back and put my seatbelt on.

"Where are we going?" I asked.

"For a ride and don't worry we will be back for your car," He responded putting the car in drive and pulling out the lot.

I sat back and enjoyed the ride and just waited to see what this mysterious man had in mind.

Chapter 10- Cobain

As I pulled out the spot and drove to the spot I was taking Ms. Keri baby I couldn't help but steal a couple of peaks at her. She was just so dam beautiful and looked so pure shit kinda reminded me of beauty and the beast.

"So, doc tell me about yourself, I see that nice rock on your finger so I know you not single," I acknowledged.

I saw her look down at her finger and start twisting her ring, then took a deep breath.

"Yeah, I'm engaged," She said in a dry tone.

"You don't sound too excited about it," I spoke.

"No, don't get me wrong. It's not that we just… just going through a rough time right now. I'm sure it will get better," She admitted.

"I'm sure it will," I replied looking over at her not really convinced at what she was saying but I knew that I would eventually break down them walls making her comfortable enough with me to open to me.

"It's not like that," She assured.

"So, tell me what it's like then," I stated.

She took a breath and looked out the window then after a few moments of silence she finally spoke.

"It's just that, Max and I have been together for about 5 years and engaged for 2, and we just not seeing eye to eye right now that's all," She tried to explain.

Before I even answered I pulled into the parking lot and cut the car off then looked at her.

"Come on doc," I told her getting out the car.

I walked around to her side and opened the door for her to get out, I held my hand out for her to grab it as she stepped out the car.

"Quite the gentleman I see," She said smiling.

"I'm what you would call a gentlethug," I stated smirking at her.

"A what?" She laughed.

"A gentlethug, I'll open the door for you and slap your ass as your walking through it," I told her honestly making her laugh out loud.

"That's very interesting," She spoke.

I interlocked my fingers in hers and led her to one of my favorite spots.

"Where are we?" She questioned looking around.

"You will see, we almost there," I responded.

Once we got close to the spot I stopped her.

"Close your eyes," I stated.

"What no," She argued.

"Close your eyes doc, I told you I got you," I assured her.

I saw the look in her eyes she really didn't want to but she did it anyway, she took once again took a breath causing me to laugh then she closed her eyes. I walked behind her and wrapped my arms around her waist and led her to my spot.

"You smell good doc," I announced.

"Thank you," She said in a soft tone.

I continued to guide her until we got to the top, once I saw that we were in a good spot I spoke.

"Open your eyes," I whispered.

"OH MY GOD THIS IS SO BEAUTIFUL," She yelled.

"I know," I responded.

I stood there with my arms wrapped around her as we overlooked the city from the top of the cliff.

"How do you know about this place?" She asked.

"When I was younger my dad used to bring me here all the time before he was murdered in a drunken road rage incident," I admitted.

"Oh my god I'm sorry," She replied in a soft tone.

"It's fine, it was a long time ago, but when I have a lot on my mind and need to think I come here and talk to him," I stated.

"Did they catch the man that killed him?" She asked.

"Yeah," I replied.

"Good, what happened to him? Did he get life in prison?" She inquired.

"Can I trust you?" I asked her seriously.

She tried to get out of my arms but I held on tighter so she couldn't turn and look at me.

"Yes… of course you can trust me," She spoke.

"I killed him," I stated.

I felt her breathing increase a little but she still didn't say anything, so I didn't either I kept looking at the city. I didn't really kill him I just wanted to see what she would say, to see if she could one day fit into my world.

"Did it haunt you? I mean after you killed him?" She asked making me bust out laughing.

"I'm just fuckin' with you doc, I didn't kill him. He ended up serving life in prison and I make sure I go up to early parole hearing that he has to make sure they keep his ass in there for the rest of his life," I told her.

"That's not funny, I thought you really killed him, I wouldn't be mad if you did though that's a lot to deal with," She acknowledged.

"Nah, but if I did and I told you could I trust you to keep it to yourself?" I questioned.

We stood there in silence none of us saying a word, just looking at the world then one word was said that came through the silence.

"Yes," Was the only word that she said and that was all I needed to hear.

"Good to know," I replied with a smile.

I pulled her over to a bench that was there and sat down next to her.

"Don't be bringing your fiancé over here to my spot in shit," I joked but was serious as fuck also.

"No... no never. I appreciate you bringing me here," She admitted.

"Do you want kids?" I quizzed.

"One day," She responded in a sad tone of voice.

"Why don't you and your fiancé have any yet if you don't mind me asking?"

"We just don't, he wants them but I'm not there yet," She stated.

I could read body language very well and I knew that I was making her uncomfortable so I decided to just drop the subject.

"Are you with your daughter's mom?" She asked catching me off guard.

"It's complicated," I admitted.

"Of course, it is," She joked.

"It's not like that," I tried to explain before getting cut off.

"It's fine really, you don't have to explain your situation to me," She said.

When I was about to say something my phone rang, I pulled it out and noticed that it was my daughter.

"Excuse me it's my daughter," I told Keri.

"No problem," She responded.

"Heyyyy princess," I said into the phone.

"Hiii daddy I miss you what are you doing?" She sang into the phone.

"I was at the mall picking you up some stuff and now I'm talking to my new friend," I told her.

"Who is your friend daddy?" She quizzed.

"You don't know her princess, but I hope you can meet her soon," I admitted looking over at Keri making her blush.

"WHO THE HELL IS THIS FRIEND YOU TELLING MY DAUGHTER ABOUT COBAIN? I KNOW YOU DON'T THINK YOU ABOUT TO HAVE SOME RANDOM AROUND MY CHILD," Shyne yelled into the phone.

"I know you done lost your dam mind yelling in my ear like that, give my daughter back the got dam phone or else," I threatened in a low tone.

I wasn't trying to show Keri this side of me now or ever for that matter, so Shyne ratchet ass getting on the phone showing her ass was something I wasn't expecting.

"Daddy are you going to bring me my stuff?" She asked in a whiny voice.

"Yes, baby girl, give me a little while then I'll be on my way," I told her.

"Okay daddy, I love youuuuuu," She sang.

"I love you too baby girl," I replied before hanging up.

I looked over at Keri who was still looking at the view, I know she heard Shyne ass on the phone but she wasn't going to comment on it.

"Sorry about that," I spoke.

"It's fine," She relied.

We sat and talked getting a little longer getting to know each other more, she was a very interesting woman that I wouldn't mind getting to know a little better. She had this real laid back take no non-sense kind of vibe. We just clicked and that was really rare for me, but I wasn't mad at it either. I saw her pull out her phone and read a message and her whole-body language changed, and I wasn't feeling that shit at all.

"What's wrong doc?" I asked getting defensive.

"Um nothing I have to go, are you ready?" She asked standing up.

"What happened?" I asked again.

"Nothing I'm fine I promise but I really need to get back to my car and get home," She urged.

I stood up and followed her as she walked back to my car without saying a word, I wasn't feeling how her whole mood just changed once she got that message. I know something was going on with her but I didn't know what, just yet but I was going to get to the bottom of it real soon. I opened the door for her and she got in and put her seatbelt on still silent.

I jumped in on myside and put the car in drive and pulled off, I drove back to the mall with both of us silent. I kept stealing glances at her and the same Keri that was with me earlier wasn't here with me right now. She kept looking at her phone and shaking her head.

"Doc you sure you okay?" I questioned again.

"Yes," She said with a smile.

I knew she was lying though because this time when she smiled at me it didn't reach her eyes. The light that was in her eyes earlier when we spoke on her life was gone and it was replaced with sadness and nervousness. We pulled back up to the mall by her car and she quickly took off her seatbelt and tried to get out the car.

"Slow down doc," I spoke.

"I'm sorry I just really need to pick up my sister and get home," She replied opening the door and getting out.

She closed the door and jumped right into her car and pulled right off, I just knew something was going on with her. I pulled out my phone and called Ali.

"Yo bro what's good?" He asked soon as he picked up.

"Can't call it, can you shoot me the doctors number?" I asked.

"Yeah, you got it. You good?" He asked in concerned tone.

"Oh, yea I'm good on that, I just wanted to make sure she was good," I responded which was somewhat the truth. She jumped out the car so dam fast I couldn't even get her number.

"Oh, aight cool I'll send it now," He responded.

"Good looks," I said hanging up the phone.

I turned my music up and let 2 Chainz talk to me as tossed my phone in my cup holder and drove to see my baby girl. I would have to see what's going on with Keri later.

Chapter 11- Ali

"When I get my hands on you. You are going to regret that shit! I'm about to murder you like I did your bitch ass son," I threatened.

"BOOM"

"NOOOOOOOOOOOOOOOOO ASHANTI," I yelled running over to her body that was now slumped over in the chair.

Just at that same moment Cobain and the crew came in guns blazing but I couldn't move, I untied her and just held her in my arms rocking back and forth.

"I'm so sorry baby, please wake up," I cried into her neck.

"Ali come on man, we gotta get out of here," Cobain said walking over to me.

"Bro look at this, how he gnna kill my baby, HOW?" I cried not caring who was around me.

"I know, but we really need to go before them boys come," He stated.

I stood up with Ashanti's lifeless body in my arms and carried her out the warehouse.

Beep... Beep... Beep...

That was my alarm going off waking me from this never-ending recurring dream, I leaned over and grabbed my phone and shut my alarm off. I laid there in my bed staring at the ceiling not ready to deal with the day. Today was the anniversary of Ashanti's death and this is the day I dreaded the most.

I got out of bed and dragged myself to the bathroom for a shower, I looked in the mirror and I could have sworn I saw Ashanti next to me giggling as she showers because I came in the bathroom to take a piss. I turned on the water and splashed some across my face, then looked at myself again and shook my head. I cut the shower on and got inside, and just stood there under the water. This day would forever be the hardest day of my life, whoever said time heals all wounds clearly didn't have to go through what I went through because this shit got harder each year and I don't see it changing no time soon. Ashanti was the love of my life and was supposed to be my wife one day and I fucked up and that one fuckup cost Ashanti her life.

 Her family didn't forgive me and I barely forgave myself, it was my job to keep her safe and I let them all down. I got out the shower and went straight to my closet, I looked up at the top and grabbed the sneaker box that was there. I went back and sat on my bed opening the box up and pulled out some pictures of Ashanti and me. We were so happy before all the bullshit happened. I took a picture out and placed it on the bed and closed the box back and put it back in the closet.

 I grabbed some black jeans and a black shirt that had red in it since red was her favorite color, and my all black Jordan's. Then walked out the closet placing my clothes on the bed, I put on my boxers and Polo T then through on my clothes, I then sprayed my Jean Claude Gaultier cologne which also Ashanti's favorite cologne on me. I picked up the picture and put it in my pocket then made my way out the house.

I shot Cobain a text letting him know what I was up to and that I was about to be missing for the day. Once that was done put my car in park and drove straight to the florist to get my girl some flowers. I turned my radio and hooked my phone up and put on her playlist that I still had in my phone of all her favorite songs. *Ariana Grande the way* was first up on the list, if anybody I knew herd this coming from my car I would surely get clowned but right now I didn't care. Today was Ashanti's day and I would only look like a sucker for her.

I stopped at the florist and picked up her favorite flowers which happen to be tulips, I got a red and yellow mix for her. I paid the cashier then made my way to the cemetery with that song on repeat. Pulling up to the cemetery I parked the car and took a deep breath, I got out and made my way over to her plot. I got to where she was buried and stood there looking at her grave, I kneeled and took the old flowers out and replaced them with the new ones I just picked up.

"Hey Shanti baby, I hope you up there resting in peace and not turning up too much, you know how you do. You up there with god dancing around to *Ariana Grande,* Real shit baby girl I miss the fuck out of you, shit hasn't been the same since you left me. I need you know that I am so sorry for failing you, I promised you that you would be safe and I fucked up and now you not here with me. I never meant for any of that to happen, I should have left you alone like you asked me to when I first tried to holla at you then you would still be here with us but I just had to have you,"

"I keep dreaming about that night and it's driving me crazy, I just need to know that you are good and that you forgive me Shanti, I think that's what's really killing me is not knowing if you forgive me. Give me a sign or something baby girl something. As you see I haven't really been dealing with too many girls, you set a bar for the next one I do take serious but that probably won't be no time soon. I love the hell out of you and probably will for the rest of my life,"

"Look I brought something for you, remember this picture of us when we went to that 90's party at the skating rink I was LL Cool J and you went as Pepa. That night was definitely one for the books, but I thought you might like the picture so I brought it for you to keep,"

I dug a small whole in front of her headstone and placed the picture in it and closed it back up. I sat there talking and apologizing for the longest hoping that she was listening to me and accepted my apology. After about an hour I decided that it was time for me to go.

"Okay Shanti, I'm about to get up out of here I'm about to go to our diner, I'll be back soon. Remember that I'll always love you,"

I kissed my hand then placed it on the top of the headstone, I took one last look at it before I turned and walked away. I got in my car and sat there for a few moments and tried to gather my thoughts before I got back on the road.

Today was all about Shanti so my next stop was her favorite diner that we would always go to no matter how bad the service was.

I started the car and pulled off still with her favorite songs blaring through the speakers.

Chapter 12- Cree

I was on my way to the diner to grab my food to go as I do every day before I head into my office, I came in there so much that as soon as they see me walk in they put my order in. I pulled into my spot and got out my car and walked inside the diner and sat at the counter and waited for my food.

"Morning Lilly girl," I greeted the waitress as she passed by me.

"Hey good morning," She replied walking pass.

"Good Morning beautiful, your food should be out in a few," Sam the owner spoke.

"Good morning Sam, no problem," I responded.

I pulled out my phone and sent Keri a text since I still haven't heard from her ass.

Me: *umm soo you don't know anybody?*

Sissy: *hey sorry I just been real busy, come by the hospital later I'll let you know when I go for lunch*

Me: *I have wrk, if you're still there when I get off I'll come by.*

Sissy: *ok ily*

Me: *ly2*

I scrolled on my phone and continued to wait on my food order to come out, I happen to look up at the door and that's when I noticed Ali walking in. He didn't even look my way he kept on walking and sat in a booth by himself. His ass was probably waiting for his little girlfriend from the salon to join him which is why he didn't acknowledge me.

I put that the back of my mind and opened Facebook and scrolled down my timeline, after a few more minutes my food was finally done. I paid for my food and was prepared to leave, I turned and looked over at Ali and saw him placing his order and that's when I noticed that Lilly only placed one glass of water down which means he was alone. I decided to go say hi before I walked out maybe he didn't notice me sitting there when he walked in.

"Hey Ali," I greeted as I got to the table.

He was scrolling in is phone and didn't even look up when I spoke, which I thought was pretty fuckin' rude. So, I decided to try again.

"Hey Morning Ali," I repeated.

"Dam man can't you see that I'm not trying to be bothered I'm over here minding my business and you steady talking. Didn't you get the hint when I didn't respond the first time," He yelled.

I stood there shocked and embarrassed that he just went off on me like that, I don't know who the fuck he thought he was talking to like that because clearly, he had me fucked up and I was about to let him know.

"First off you smug dread head bastard I don't know who the fuck you think you talking to but I'm not one of your little stupid hoes that you think you can talk to any ol kinda way and I'm going to accept it. All I did was come say good morning and you wanna act like a jackass so fuck you I hope your stupid rude ass chokes on your breakfast and they CPR can't save you," I yelled walking out.

"Yo," I heard from behind me.

I kept on walking out the door to my car, he had some fuckin' nerve with his ugly ass looking like Sanka from the movie *Cool Runnings*. I jumped in my car and started up and was about to pull off until I heard a knock on my window.

"What the fuck do you want?" I asked with so much attitude.

"I just wanna apologize ma, that wasn't even me back there," He stated.

"I don't care who I was and I don't accept your whack ass apology," I threw back at him.

"Dam ma it's like that?" He said sounding like I hurt his feelings.

"Yea it is and stop calling me ma, cuz that isn't my name," I stated in a matter of fact tone.

"Cree, I would like to formally apologize for how I came at you back there, I'm not myself today and that was pretty fucked up of me to take it out on you. Now will you please accept my apology?" He asked in the sincerest tone.

"NOPE," I replied and pulled off.

He clearly didn't know what kind of female I was and I didn't take well to disrespect at all. I pulled up to my job grabbed my foot from the passenger seat and walked into my office.

"Good Morning everyone," I greeted walking into the office.

"Morning Cree," Ming the secretary greeted with a smile along with everyone else

I walked to my office and closed my door and sat behind my desk, I already had a headache and my dad hasn't even started yet. I opened my food and dug in as I started to go over a few designs from yesterday that I still wasn't sure about. I picked up a pencil and started sketching some new ideas that I thought the perspective client would like even better then what I previously showed them.

Knock... Knock...

"Come in," I announced never looking up from my papers.

"Hey Cree, sorry for interrupting you, but I just wanted to let you know your 11am appointment cancelled and said that they would be calling you back when they had a new time to meet with you," She told me.

I dropped my pencil and just that fast I was annoyed, I really hated when they did that shit.

"Thank you, Ming," I replied.

"No problem, oh and you have a new perspective client, here is the information," She responded handing me the sticky paper.

"Okay, thank you," I said taking the paper.

She walked out closing the door behind her, since I didn't have to finish the designs right away I decided to finish my breakfast before I had to go meet my potential new client. I grabbed my design book and a few pencils and tossed them in my bag and grabbed the sticky note and left my office.

I got in my car and put the address in my GPS and made my way to the client's house. I decided to play some Bishop T.D Jakes on the way there. I wouldn't say I was depressed but I was thinking what was wrong with me for me to be attracting these seeming less perfect guys then they all turn out to be fuckboys in disguise.

I pulled up to the address and put all my problems in my life to the back of my mind and got back into professional mode, I took a breath and got out the car. I looked around and the house was nice from the outside great landscaping and a beautiful red door.

I was cursing myself now for not getting the client's name from Ming before running out the office. I rang the bell and waited for someone to come answer it, I looked at my watch and I saw that I was a few minutes early. Finally, I heard the doors unlock and open and I was instantly pissed at who the owner was.

"Hello Cree and thank you for coming, please come in," Ali said standing to the side so that I could come in.

"I'm not doing this with you today, you called my job? How the hell did you even know where I worked? You know what it don't even matter because I can't help you. I'll recommend someone else for you," I told him walking back down the steps.

"I personally asked for you, now if you don't help me I will have to call your boss and complain and I know you wouldn't want that," He stated with a smirk on his face that I wanted to slap off.

I turned around and went back in the house pissed the hell off that he would do something like this.

"I knew you would see things my way," He spoke.

"Whatever what's the room that I'm here to look at?" I asked looking around at the place.

"Right this way," He said walking away.

I followed behind him looking at each of the rooms that we passed the house was already in immaculate condition so I'm not sure what I was even doing here in the first place. We walked up the stairs and stopped at the last door at the end of the hall. When he opened the door, I saw the most amazing bedroom that I've seen in a long time.

"Is this some kind of joke?" I asked as I walked into the bedroom.

"Nope, I need you to work on my room It, doesn't scream me," He said shrugging his shoulders.

I took out my notepad and took a few notes as I continued to make my rounds of the room.

"What would you want to change now?" I quizzed looking at him.

"For one the color It just feels stale to me and in need you to make it feel like me. I don't care the price just make it happen," He stated.

"Got it," I replied still scribbling on my pad.

"Cool, do you know the timeframe?" He asked.

"Let's set up a meeting so I can get to know you a little better and feel you out then I can get some ideas drawn up for you," I suggested.

"Copy," He replied.

"Will there be anything else?" I asked putting my stuff in my bag.

"Actually yes, listen about earlier," He started to say.

"Listen earlier was just that I don't really, -" I said before getting cut off.

"Just listen, earlier I wasn't myself, and when you came to the table I wasn't all the way there yet. If you want me to keep it real not a lot of people know but today is the anniversary of the day I lost someone very important to me, so when I walked into the diner I had just come from their grave," He admitted instantly making me feel like shit.

"I'm so sorry for your loss Ali, if I would have none I would have never went off on you like that," I spoke truthfully.

"It cool, I was very rude and disrespectful so I deserved it," He stated.

"It was and I shouldn't have pushed you, and for that I apologize also," I explained.

"Now do you accept my apology?" He asked bringing his hands up in a pleading manner making me laugh.

"Yes, I do," I said through laughter.

"Good a nigga thought he was going to have to makeover the whole house before you forgave me," He chuckled.

"You would have done that?" I asked shockingly.

"Hell yea, you know you about to be my bae. I gotta make sure your pockets stay on full," He said in a matter of fact tone.

"Any way, if that's all I need to get back to the office," I acknowledged ignoring what he just he just said.

"Don't ignore me, you know before today I was checking you out every time I saw you," He said.

"Yeah okay, that don't mean anything," I said as I walked out the bedroom.

"That means a lot coming from me because I don't check out nobody that I don't feel like is on my level some way or another," He spoke.

"I hear you, so when do you want to meet up again to go over these designs?" I asked.

"I'll call you," He stated.

"Wait about that, how did you even know where I worked?" I quizzed.

"I text Keri and told her that I had fucked up with you and needed to make it up to you and she gave me your number," He admitted.

"I'm going to get her oh my god," I screeched shaking my head.

"If it makes a difference she really didn't want to but I have my ways to persuade people," He smirked.

"I don't care she still shouldn't have told you, she doesn't know if you were trying to kill me or anything," I stated seriously.

"Man shut your dramatic ass up," He laughed.

"Whatever, call me when you ready to discuss your bedroom," I told him as I opened the door.

"Cree, let me take you out on a date not business related," He spoke in a serious tone.

"Honestly, I don't think that would be a good idea," I admitted.

"Why not?" He questioned.

"I'm just not looking to date anyone right now,"

"Listen ma I'm not saying we are going down to the wedding chapel and eloping I'm saying we can hit up a Friday's and get them ten-dollar appetizers and half off drinks, some real simple shit. I just wanna get to know you, I've been liking your style since the first night I seen you in the hospital," He admitted grabbing my hand.

I stood there and looking at him and debating if I should really go out with this man, my bad luck streak I'm sure isn't over yet and I really wasn't in the mood to be embarrassed again.

"Come on pretty lady Cree just one date," He said bringing me from my thoughts holing up my pointer finger looking at me waiting for confirmation.

"Fine, don't make me regret this," I said pulling my hand from his and getting in my car.

I looked up at him and he was standing in the doorway with a smile on his face just looking stupid as can be. I started the car and drove off, just hoping that I didn't make a mistake agreeing to go on a date with him.

Chapter 13- Keri

After getting into my car I raced back to my mom house and went to get Khloe only to find out that Max stopped by my mom's house and picked her up already. I knew it was some shit that was about to go down now, that explains why he was calling me like that.

"FUCKKKKKKKKKK" I yelled banging on the steering wheel as the tears fell from my face.

I knew there was something that I was going to have to do about Khloe because I can't keep living like this. I got to my house and slowly got out my car, I took slow steady breaths as I walked up to the door. I stuck my key in the door and tried to open it only for it not to open.

"What the fuck," I mumbled to myself.

I started banging on the door and ringing the bell, only for nobody to answer the door. I pulled my phone out my bag and dialed Max's number.

"Hello, Max baby, what's going on why isn't my key opening the door?" I asked as calmly as possible.

"Good evening dear, I see you finally made it home. Well your key isn't working because I changed the locks on the door," He spoke in a casual tone.

"Huh? What do you mean you changed the locks and where is Khloe?" I questioned.

"Khloe and I are getting dinner, I wanted to surprise you but imagine the surprise I got when I went by your mother's place and you weren't even there with Khloe," He spoke in a taunting tone.

"Max, - "I spoke.

"Save it Keri, we will discuss it when I get home. So, make sure your there when we get home," He stated hanging up the phone.

"AHHHHHHHHHHHHH," I yelled out.

I was so fuckin frustrated with him, I went and at back in my car and cried. This isn't the life I pictured for myself when Max got down on one knee and proposed to me.

When we first met he was always the perfect gentleman and then one day he just woke up and changed into this person that I don't even know anymore.

Max and I met six years ago at a banquet given by the hospital to help raise money for kids with cancer and then they donate it to St. Jude's hospital. I was there with Cree of course and he was there with his job and it's like when we first locked eyes it was love at first sight, of course I had to play hard to get but eventually he won me over and we've been together ever since. At first, he was a perfect gentleman and the most loving man I've ever dealt with, then over time he became this monster that I didn't even recognize and now I hated him and with my whole being.

I sat in my car texting Cree trying to take my mind off my current fucked up situation. She was fake pissed that I gave Ali her information but I had to, he was so upset that he hurt her like that and from the sound of his voice it really fucked with him that she didn't accept his apology. So, who was I to not help him out in his time of need, she can be mad all she wants but Ali is good for her. I don't know much about him but from my standpoint they are perfect for each other.

Knock… Knock…

I looked up and saw Max knocking on the window of my car with his demonic eyes. I slowly opened my door and he held his hand out for me to grab. I grabbed his hand and stepped out the car, he squeezed my hand so hard that I thought he was going to break it.

"Hello dear," He spoke as he brought my hand up to his lips and kissed it.

"Hi guys," I replied as Max still squeezed my hand.

"Hey Keri," Khloe said.

"Max you're hurting me," I whispered with a fake smile on my face as I looked over at Khloe.

He didn't respond he just kept a smile on his face, I closed my door and let him pull me to the house. I watched as Khloe used her keys to open the door and I looked over at Max and he still had this grin on his face.

"Thanks for dinner Max," Khloe said as soon as we walked in the house.

"Of course, Khloe thanks for joining me," He replied.

Max still had my hand as we headed to our bedroom, once we got there he closed the door and finally let go off my hand.

"Where were you Keri?" He angrily asked.

"I was driving around I needed to clear my head after talking to my mom," I admitted as I rubbed my hand.

"So, if that's the case why didn't you pick up when I called? He questioned walking closer to me making me back up.

"I left my phone in the car, I went to the pier and left my whole bag inside the car," I spoke.

"Hmm, really?" He replied.

"Yes Max,"

"So why didn't you call Khloe when you got to your mom's house and saw she wasn't there?" He questioned.

"When I got there and saw she wasn't there without my mom even having to tell me, I knew you came and got her," I explained.

He walked in the closet leaving me standing on edge, I hated when he did shit like this to me.

"Max what happened to us?" I questioned.

"We are fine Keri," He stated walking out the closet.

"Fine Max really, you call this fine?" I yelled.

"Watch it," He threatened.

"Max, it's such a mystery when you're here with me, this isn't how it's supposed to be," I stated.

"Well what do you want me to say Keri huh, you know it's a lot going with work and I'm stressed and what do you to help me? NOTHING, ALL YOU DO IS ADD MORE STRESS TO MY ALREADY STRESSED LIFE," He yelled in a harsh whisper.

"How would I know what you're going through when you don't talk to me Max, all you do is raise a hand to me like I'm your child and I'm tired Max I'm tired of it and it has to stop," I told him with tears in my eyes.

He looked at me and for a minute I thought I saw a glimmer of hope but that quickly disappeared.

"Keri your right once the pressure at work eases up, I will be back to the old Max. I will try hard not to hit you anymore, I can't make any promises that it won't happen again because it just might. My dad used to hit my mom all the time and they have been married for thirty years, she didn't leave so why are you Keri? You think your better than my mom?" He questioned with mad eyes.

"That's not even what I'm saying Max stop twisting my words around, I'm just saying I don't know how much longer I can put up with this… this love is taking all of my energy. I'm just asking if you can work on not hitting me anymore," I pleaded with him.

He looked at me and didn't respond, instead he walked up to me and kissed me on the forehead.

"Goodnight my love," He spoke then hit the lights and got in the bed leaving me standing there in the dark.

I walked into my closet and took off my clothes and put on some pajamas then went in the bathroom and washed my face. Before walking out the bathroom I said a silent prayer to god that things didn't get any worse before they got better. I walked out the bathroom and got in the bed and gave Max my back.

"Keri," He spoke.

"Yes Max," I replied.

"Do that thing I like," He requested.

I held back my tears and took a breath and turned over and faced him and did what he asked of me.

Chapter 14- Cobain

I can't believe how Keri just jumped out my car and pulled off like that, it was definitely something going on with her and I was going to get to the bottom of it one way or another. I pulled up to Shyne's house and grabbed Kaylee's things and got out. I walked to the door and rang the bell, I had the key since I was paying the bills here but I wanted to let her know that I wasn't on that wave with her anymore.

"Why you didn't just use your key?" She questioned as soon as she opened the door.

"Because at the end of the day this is your house and I'm going to respect it as such," I stated.

"I guess," She replied moving over so I could come in.

I walked in and looked around at the place and it was always clean, I was happy that she wasn't like them other baby mother's that I use to hear stories about from a few of my boys. Even though she could be annoying as fuck at times I really lucked up with her.

"Where's baby girl?" I questioned.

"She in the living room watching TV," She responded.

I walked into the living and just stared at my baby girl, she was so dam pretty a perfect blend of the both of us. She was just so perfect to me, she could have the whole world if she wanted it. She was so into her show she didn't even notice me standing there watching as she sang along to her shows.

"You must really love this show huh," I spoke.

She stopped and turned and looked at me and her eyes lit up, she jumped off the couch and ran and jumped on me.

"DADDDDYYYYY," She screamed squeezing me tight.

"Mmmmmmm, hi baby girl," I replied squeezing her back.

"I didn't think I would be seeing you today," She said into my neck.

"I told you I would, do I ever let you down?" I asked making her look me in the eyes.

"No daddy," She said hugging me again.

"And I never will," I responded.

"What did you get me?" She inquired as she wiggled her way out my arms.

I handed her the bags and she dropped on the floor right there and opened everything screaming as she went through each one.

"OH MY GOD DADDY I LOVE EVERYTHING, YOU'RE THE BEST DADDY EVER," She spoke in a dramatic voice.

"I'm glad you like it princess," I responded with a smile.

Doing anything for her always kept me in a positive mood, she was so easy to keep happy I didn't understand how people were deadbeats with their kids, they didn't require much at all. I was helping her put her dollhouse together when Shyne came in the living room.

"Hey, you are staying for dinner?" She asked.

"Ummm,"

"Please stay daddy please please, please," Kaylee begged with her puppy dog eyes and pouty lip.

"Yeah, I'll stay," I gave in and said.

"YAAAYYYY," Kaylee cheered.

We sat there singing along to the TV and trying to finish putting together her house, this shit had so many dam pieces I don't know what the fuck I was thinking even getting her this shit. I was over it as soon as she dumped it out the box.

"Dinner is ready," Shyne called from the kitchen.

"Come on Kaylee let's go wash our hands," I told her dropping that dam doll so fast.

We both got up and went to the bathroom to wash our hands for dinner, while we were in the bathroom Kaylee started to whisper.

"Daddy I want to come live you," She whispered.

"You know you always can but what's wrong why don't you wanna stay with mommy anymore?" I questioned not sure where this came from all of a sudden.

"You promise you won't tell mommy? I don't want to get in trouble," She said in a scared tone which had me heated as fuck.

"I promise baby girl," I told her even though I already knew that Shyne was about to be put in her place.

"I do it just that earlier mommy said if you had a new friend I wasn't going to be allowed to see you anymore," She admitted making my blood boil.

"Kaylee listen to me you don't ever have to worry about not ever seeing me, because that will never happen," I stated in a serious tone.

"Okay, daddy," She replied in shaky tone.

I kissed her forehead and we continued to wash our hands then head into the dining room for dinner. I pulled

Kaylee's chair out and let her sit down before I sat down next to her, Shyne already had our plates made.

"Kaylee, you want to say grace baby?" Shyne asked her.

"Okay mommy," She responded.

We all grabbed hands and bowed our heads as she started saying grace.

"God is grace, god is good thank you for this food that we are about to receive, amen," She recited.

"Amen," We all said.

We all started to eat and I had to admit shit was good, Shyne always knew how to throw down in the kitchen like someone's old ass southern grandmother. No matter how hard Shyne tried she just didn't meet my wants and needs, and she thought that just because she had my daughter that automatically made her my woman and that was far from the truth.

"How are you feeling Cobain since you've been home?" Shyne asked.

"Honestly, I feel good can't complain," I spoke before I put some food in my mouth.

"Good" She replied with a smirk.

I wanted to slap that grin off her stupid ass face for telling my daughter that shit but it's cool we was going to have our time as soon as baby girl went to sleep. Even though Keri didn't know it but she was about to be mine, and Shyne was going to have to understand that or get dealt with.

"Daddy do you still have pain?" Kaylee asked sounding so innocent.

"A little but if I do I just take some medicine and the pain goes away," I responded with a smile.

We all continued to make small talk at the dinner table mostly Kaylee though telling us what she wanted for her birthday which was about six months away. For the most part, the dinner was a good one. While Shyne cleaned the kitchen, I helped Kaylee bring all her toys upstairs and out the living room.

"Daddy after mommy helps bathe me can you stay and tuck me then read me a story before you go?" She asked.

"Anything for you baby girl, you know that," I stated.

"Good, I'm going to get my stuff out and go start my bath, stay in my room daddy," She told me.

"Okay Kaylee," I laughed.

I pulled out my phone and started to send Keri a text to make sure she was good, but I quickly decided against it. I was going to give her a few days then text her to let her know that I was thinking about her. I didn't know much about her but what I did know was that I needed her on my team and I always get what I want.

"I'm back daddyyyyyy," Kaylee came in the room singing.

"Don't you look pretty, I love your pajama set baby girl,"

"Thank you, mommy, got it for me," She said climbing in the bed.

"Well mommy did a good job with that one," I smirked as I pulled the covers up on her.

"Daddy can you get the book off my bookshelf please," She asked grinning.

"Um and why didn't you grab it before you got in the bed silly girl?" I asked tickling her/

"I don't know," She cried out through her laughter.

I got up and walked to the shelf picking up the book, I don't even know why she wanted me to get this book. She knew the whole book by heart, I've been reading the same book since she could talk, but just like her mother she liked the dramatic effects of having the book in my hands. I sat down next to her and started to read.

I watched her face as I read each page to her and it was always like a new book to her each time. I was so grateful that I was still here for this because I almost wasn't, so I was cherishing this time as well as any other time that was to come. I saw her little eyes were closed and I closed the book leaned over and kissed her forehead then got up and hit the lights before walking out of her room making sure to close the door behind me.

I walked into Shyne's bedroom and there she was laying across her bed in a red lingerie number with her pussy exposed. Her body was on point, she made sure she stayed in the gym after she had Kaylee. I'm not even going to lie a nigga dick was hard as fuck but the shit she said to my daughter wouldn't leave my mind, so I was about to show her a lesson.

"Hey baby, I was waiting for you," She cooed in a sultry voice.

I walked further in her room and closed the door behind me, and just stood there and watched her as she started to play in her pussy.

"Ssssssss," She moaned as she went faster in her pussy.

"Keep playing with that pussy," I coached as I dropped my jeans and boxers and started stroking my dick.

"Ahhhhhh Cobain baby, I wanna feel you inside of me," She panted.

She moved her fingers all around her pussy making herself cum all over her fingers them pulling her hand from her pussy and licking the cum off her fingers. She had my dick hard as fuck and I needed to get this nut out.

"Come get this nut," I spoke in a low tone.

She had the look of lust in her eyes as she slowly crawled off the bed and made her way over to me. She tried to kiss me and I turned my head and let her kiss my neck instead, I grabbed on her fat ass and squeezed it and she kept kissing on me.

"Suck my dick bae," I told her.

She looked at me and bit her bottom lip before slowly going down and putting me all the way in her mouth.

"Shit," I moaned out.

I had to bite down on my knuckle as she went to work on my dick, she was deep throating the fuck out of my dick making a nigga knees weak as fuck causing me to fall back on the wall.

"Dam I miss this dick," She said in between kisses.

I grabbed the back of her head and started fucking her face, she had so much spit coming from her mouth the dam side of my legs were wet along with my boxers. She pulled away and started working on my balls.

"Ahhhhhhh Ssssssss fuck Shyne," I groaned like a little bitch making her suck on my balls a little harder.

She started playing in her pussy as she continued to suck me off, she came back to my dick and started sucking it faster and harder. I started to feel my nut building so I grabbed the back of her head again and started fuckin' her mouth harder until I came all in her mouth.

"AHHHHHHHHHHHHHH,"

I pulled her head back and she looked up at me with a smirk.

"Swallow and say ah," I told her.

She swallowed and then opened her mouth and stuck her tongue out showing me that her mouth was open.

"Really Cobain that's how you doing it now?" She asked in a shocked tone as I was walking to the bathroom.

"Really you low key sneaky and I'm not trying to get caught up with you like that," I stated truthfully grabbing a washcloth and washing my dick off in her sink before pulling my pants up.

"So, we can't fuck? I'm horny Cobain," She whined.

"I can't help you with that shorty, play with your pussy again," I said shrugging my shoulders.

"You make me sick asshole," She yelled.

"Tell me something I don't know,"

"Whatever," She replied walking into the bathroom and slamming the door.

"Don't be mad at me because your little pussy is hot and ready like a little Caesar pizza and you can't handle it," I joked as I sat on her bed waiting for her to come out the bathroom.

"Shut the fuck up," She screamed from in the bathroom.

I pulled out my phone and started handling some business as I heard the shower cut on. I waited for her stupid ass to come out the bathroom so I could go do what I needed to do. Finally, after about forty-five fuckin minutes I finally heard the water turn off. The bathroom door swung open and she stood there with her short silk robe on drying her hair with a towel.

"What the fuck took your ass so dam long?" I asked annoyed as fuck.

"For one I didn't even know your ass was still here and for two I had to wash my hair and get myself off again since my stupid ass baby daddy didn't fuck me," She stated.

"Yeah kill all that shit you talking right now, let me run something by you right quick," I spoke.

"What?" She asked.

"Did you or did you not tell Kaylee that if I had another friend you wouldn't let her see me no more? And before you think about calling my daughter a liar DON'T," I threatened.

"Cobain listen," She started.

"DID YOU, OR DIDN'T YOU?" I barked causing her to jump a little

"Yes," She admitted.

"Now why would you do something like that Shyne? Don't I make sure your account is full? Don't I pay all your bills? Don't you not want for NOTHING? So why would you tell my daughter some shit like?" I questioned.

"I didn't really mean it I was just mad at the shit you said earlier," She admitted.

"But why though? we aren't together and haven't been in a long time, so why would you feel away about anything I tell her?" I inquired.

"Wow, are you that blind Cobain? Why do you think? I'm still on love with you. I've been in love with you since the day I first laid eyes on you and that's never going to change," She explained.

"Listen all that shit you saying right now is all cool and shit but the real is do I love you yes I do but only as the mother of my daughter nothing more nothing less,"

"But why?' She begged on the brink of tears.

"It's just what it is Shyne, I don't know what else you want me to tell you," I stated.

"Get out my house," She cried.

"That's cool, I'll leave but remember what I said if you want to keep up this lifestyle don't fuck with me and my daughter, because real shit baby mama or not I'll makes you disappear and have Kaylee calling someone else mommy," I told her looking her right in the eyes before walking out.

"FUCK YOU," She screamed.

I walked down the hallway looked in on Kaylee one last time before leaving her house. One thing for sure, two things for certain I didn't play when it came to my daughter and everybody who was anybody knew that about me. I didn't have a problem getting rid of anybody that stood in my way of being a father, Shyne included.

Chapter 15- Ali

Two weeks later

"Ayo, what's good bro," I greeted as I walked into Cobain's crib.

"What's good nigga what you doing here?" He asked.

"Dam I can't see how my brother is doing? I gotta have a reason to stop by now?" I questioned playing hurt.

"Nah not at all you already know you always welcome here," He replied.

We walked into the living room and sat down, he put the TV on mute and faced me.

"So, what's up? I know you long enough to know that something is on your mind," He stated.

I looked at him and it killed me that he always knew when something was on my mind or if I was going through something. I knew I couldn't keep this from him any longer then I already have.

"Aight this is the deal, the night you got shot a nigga fucked up," I admitted.

"What you mean you fucked up?" He asked.

"Dragon got away," I stated.

"WHAT THE FUCK MAN, DAM, WHY YOU JUST NOW TELLING ME THIS SHIT," He barked.

"I know I fucked up,"

"Yeah you did, this is something that you should have told me when I first woke up, instead of having me out here blind and shit," He explained.

"Nah you right, I thought I could handle it while you healed. I had eyes on him but now the mother fucker just up and disappeared," I explained.

"FUCKKKKKKK Ali," He said hitting the wall.

"I know, but I have the team on round the clock surveillance looking for him and we have people watching his family, so I'm on it," I acknowledged.

"I get that bro, I just wish you would have told me sooner so I would have been more prepared instead of out here walking around like a big ass target," He stated.

"Yeah you right my fault," I apologized.

"Is there anything else you need to tell me?' He asked sarcastically.

"Nah that's it,"

"Good, don't stress yourself to much over that, I know you did everything you could that night and I still owe you for that, real shit, you saved my life," He said sincerely.

"Nah you don't owe me shit because if the shoe was on the other foot you would have done the same for me," I spoke straight up.

We sat and talked trying to put a plan together to catch this son of a bitch and end this shit for good. After the business part was done with we started getting back to the personal shit.

"What's the plans for the day?" Cobain inquired as he drank his beer.

"I'm taking Cree little chocolate ass out to eat," I said with a grin on my face.

"Oh shit, how you swing that, I didn't even know y'all was talking," He responded.

I got to telling him about the situation at the diner and how I blacked on her and shit, so I had to make it up to her.

"Dam, nigga I forgot it was the anniversary of Shanti, may my sis continue R.I.P.," He spoke.

"Right," I replied.

"Fuck you didn't tell me for I would have went with you, I needed to talk to Shanti ol big headed ass," He joked.

"I should have but I needed to see her alone, a nigga been having them dreams again and I needed to make sure she was good," I admitted.

"Dam nigga I keep telling you to go see someone about those, you don't listen for shit," He snapped.

"Chill nigga dam. I did speak to someone, I spoke to Ashanti. So hopefully now that the anniversary is done I should be good now," I stated.

"Whatever nigga," He replied.

"Anyway, where are you taking Cree?" He asked changing the subject.

"I told her little ass we were going to Friday's," I said shrugging my shoulders.

"I know your ass wasn't serious about that shit," He laughed.

"Yes, the hell I was, I'm already spending money on my crib for her little ass to fix up since I initially fucked up. So, she better takes these ten-dollar appetizers and be happy," I chuckled.

"You stupid as fuck," He said in between laughing.

"Whatever, what's going on with you and the doctor? I asked changing the subject.

"I don't know it's something with her though I just need to figure it out, but besides her being beautiful she's cool as fuck to be around," He told me.

"That's what's up, hopefully what she has going on isn't too much," I stated.

"Right, but I'm going to find out," He said in a matter of fact tone.

"Knowing you I already know you are," I laughed.

"Ya dam right," He replied laughing.

We sat there chopping it up a little while longer until it was time for me to go meet Cree for lunch.

"Aight bro, let me go get this girl," I said as I got up.

"Cool, be safe. Hit me later," He told me.

"Will do," I replied walking out his house.

***

I pulled up to Cree's apartment and shot her a text letting her know that I was downstairs, when I saw her come outside a nigga was stuck. She was looking so dam beautiful, and that was putting it lightly, shorty was bad as fuck and all natural. She actually had me get out of my car to open the door for her just so I could get a better look at her.

"Dam ma, I mean Cree. You are looking good as fuck right now," I told her truthfully causing her chocolate skin to blush.

"Thank you," She responded.

"I'm saying though a nigga got out to open the door for you can I get a hug?" I quizzed.

"Nope," She replied getting in the car.

I closed the door behind her and shook my head at her slick ass I bet by the end of the night she was going to be hugging me fuck she thought. I walked to the other side got in and pulled off. The first few minutes of the ride were quiet until she finally decided to speak.

"So, when you first mentioned this date I thought it would have been like that week or weekend the latest but here we are two weeks later finally going on this date," She spoke.

"Man cut it out we BOTH have been busy, you are acting like I wasn't facetiming your ass every night before you went to bed or we weren't talking throughout the day," I stated in a matter of fact tone.

"That's not the point though." She laughed.

"I already see it."

"See what?" She questioned looking over at me.

"That your little ass is soiled as fuck and need attention," I explained.

"No, I'm not," She replied in a childlike voice.

"It's cool though, I don't mind spoiling your sexy ass," I stated glancing over at her.

We continued making small talk as I drove to the restaurant, Cree was really cool and I was enjoying our conversations, everything was just flowing so naturally.

"OH, SHIT THIS MY SONG," She shrieked cutting up the music.

"Now what the hell your bougie ass know about some dam Migos?" I asked laughing at her as she started dancing in her seat.

"I'll have you know I'm not bougie, I'm sophistiratchet," She stated.

"Man, what the hell is sophistiratchet?" I asked through laughter.

"Don't laugh at me that's a real word," She insisted.

"So, what's the definition?" I asked.

"It's a woman that's highly educated pedigree VIA academically, socially and otherwise. She's fluent in various forms of public etiquette, yet is equally knowledgeable of the latest strip club songs and updated on most of the ratchet television shows. I can waltz at a ball or twerk with the best of em," She smirked.

"You made that shit up, I don't care what the hell you over here think you talking about," I told her.

"Whatever check out the dictionary bruh shit is real," She laughed.

I continued to sneak glances from the corner of my eye as she rapped along to Miegos, shorty definitely had it going on and was about to be on my team sooner rather than later. A few minutes later we were pulling up to the Fridays by the mall and she looked around then at me.

"You really brought me to Fridays? She asked with the stink face?'

"What your sophistiratchet ass too good for Friday's?" I questioned with a smirk.

"Nope not at all," She replied smiling.

"Good," I chuckled.

"Just don't think I'm getting no dam ten-dollar appetizers and half off drinks either," She said as she got out the car causing me to laugh out loud.

"I hear you,"

"I hope you hear this appetizer, entrée, and desert that I'm about to order on top of a few drinks too," She stated folding her arms.

"That's fine, I can afford it all," I shrugged putting my arm around her as we made our way to the door.

"Hi table for two please, a booth if you have," I told the hostess.

"No problem, right this way," She responded.

We both followed the hostess to the table and had a seat.

"Thank you," We both said in unison.

The waitress walked away leaving us alone, Cree opened her menu and scanned through it. I just studied her, she was so graceful with a splash of hood in her.

"I like your hair better this way," I said randomly.

"Huh?" She looked up at me with a confused look.

"Your hair, I like the natural look better than that dam fake shit you had when you came to my place," I told her.

"Oh, thank you, I was just trying something different," She explained.

"Well don't," I told her.

"You aint my dam daddy," She mumbled.

"I could be," I looked at her and blew a kiss.

"Speaking off being someone's daddy, who was ol girl that was at the salon that day I saw you?" She asked.

"Why you jealous?" I questioned.

"Who me? Never have I ever been jealous of anyone in my life," She stated.

"Cocky huh?" I joked.

"That's right I'm cocky and confident, and not to be played with" She told me.

"I hear you Cree," I said touching her hand.

"So?" She asked moving her hand from me and folding her arms.

"So, what?"

"Who was ol' girl? I don't have time for games and I'm too old for drama. So, if that's your girl just let me know. I'll rather the truth then a lie any day," She said looking me in the eyes.

"For starters, I don't lie nor do I cheat if I'm committed to you then I'm committed only to you, second that girl in the shop was my little cousin Jessica that I helped her mom take care of since her bitch ass daddy left her years ago. Third I haven't been a real relationship in a few years, so if you ever heard that shorty is lying. I might fuck you here and there but that's about it, and you not even welcome to my house and that's the real," I told her straight up.

"Wow, good to know," She spoke.

The waitress came over and we both placed our food and drink orders then handed her back the menu.

"That's it? Just good to know?" I questioned.

"Yeah, what else am I supposed to say?" She giggled.

"I don't know, you caught me off guard with that response," I told her.

"Listen I'm not like those other girls where I'm going to badger and annoy you for answers. If you tell me something that's what it is until you show me otherwise, you say that's your cousin cool. I believe you. Simple," She explained.

"I think I'm in love," I joked laughing.

"Shut up," She laughed.

"Nah I'm fuckin' with you but that's real and I can't even be mad at you. I respect that, real shit," I spoke.

"So why haven't you been in a quote on quote real relationship?" She asked me changing my whole mood.

The waitress came back over with our food and drinks and walked away leaving us alone again. I took a deep breath and started telling her about the story of Ashanti and me. By the time I was done she had tears in her eyes and I dropped a few tears but quickly wiped them.

"I'm so sorry for your loss Ali," She said in the sincerest voice squeezing my hand.

"It's cool," I downplayed.

"It's not cool," She replied wiping her eyes.

"Yea I just take it one day at a time, but always around her anniversary I get these nightmares and I wake up in a cold sweat," I admitted.

"Have you tried talking to someone about these nightmares?" She asked me.

"Nah, because I'm good," I spoke.

"When is her anniversary?" She inquired.

"The day you saw me in the diner, I had just come from her gravesite. It always puts me in a sour mood hence why I flipped on you. Again, I apologize for that," I told her sincerely.

"No, it's cool you don't have to apologize anymore, I shouldn't have been so pushy that day," She replied.

The next few minutes were spent in silent as we ate our food, it wasn't an awkward silence it was actually really comfortable which I enjoyed.

"So, tell me how long you've known the doctor?" I asked finally breaking the silence.

"Oh my god Keri and I have known each other pretty much our whole lives, we go back like criss cross and hopscotch," She laughed.

"Word that's what's up, and y'all both about business which is a good thing," I stated.

"Yeah that's my girl, I love her to death and would do anything for her," She said with a smile.

"What about you and your brother?" She asked.

"Man, me and him go back to high school days, that's my brother for life. We like *Will Smith* and *Martin Lawrence* from the movie *Bad Boys*. If you see him I'm never too far behind always remember that," I stated.

"Bad Boys huh, you Will or Martin?" She asked as she started to laugh.

"Will of course fuck you thought," I replied poppin' my collar.

We sat the rest of the time laughing and talking just having a really good time, it was rare that I laughed this much out with a female and not been bored. Cree was something special I could see it already. I knew I was going to have to snatch her up fast.

"So, tell me Ms. Cree why are you single? I mean your obviously beautiful and a great catch. So, help me figure this out" I quizzed.

"Well I just haven't found the right person for me yet, lately the guys that I've been meeting have been leaving a bad taste in my mouth. Like HORRIBLE. So, I kind of fell back. Keri told me to just sit back and let him find me but how can he find me if I'm not out there you know?" She explained.

"I get it, and I'm sorry if the fuck boys you dealt with left a sour taste in your mouth, but I'm here to tell you that from this moment on you won't have to deal with another lame again," I told her honestly.

"Oh really? And why is that?" She asked with the raise of an eyebrow.

"Because you got me now, and I don't like to share what's mine is mine, and if anybody has an issue with that tell them come see me and I'll be glad to help them fix it," I spoke seriously.

"Is that so?"

"It is," I replied as I stroked my beard.

"I hear you," She smirked.

We finally finished our food I paid the bill and we left, I grabbed her hand as we walked to the car. It was weird since I haven't held a female's hand since Ashanti, but it felt natural. I don't know where we would end up but I know this wasn't the last time that we would be around each other if I had a say in it.

Chapter 16- Keri

I was supposed to go to work today but I ended up switching shifts with another doctor so I was going to do an overnight so that I wouldn't have to deal with Max tonight. He was becoming too much now, at first, I could handle it but now it's becoming overwhelming to say the least and I needed a break away from him even if it was just work. So today I had a planned to go by Cree's place and pig out with her and have a bunch of much needed girl talk.

I dropped Khloe to one of her friend's house they were going to the movies then she was going to spend the night with them while I was at work, so I didn't have to worry about her with at home while Max was on one of his drunken nights. I went to the supermarket and picked up a few of our favorite snacks and a few bottles of wine and was ready to start our day.

I used my key and let myself in her house making sure to close the door behind me. I walked in her kitchen and placed the groceries on the counter and went and looked around to see where Cree was.

"Cree?" I called out as I walked upstairs.

Still nothing I noticed her door was closed so I knocked first and waited for a response but still got nothing.

"Cree?" I knocked again.

When I still got nothing, I opened the door and peeked my head inside.

"Cree wake up it's not that early and your usually up before me," I spoke walking in and opening the blinds to shine some light in the room.

I turned about to jump on her when I noticed she wasn't alone.

"OH, SHIT CREE," I yelled.

"KERIIIII GET OUT OH MY GOD," She screamed as she covered her face.

"My fault sis," I replied laughing and walking out her room closing the door behind me.

I walked back downstairs and went in the kitchen and poured me a glass of wine for this shit I just saw. A few minutes later I heard footsteps coming down the steps and walking into the kitchen.

"Good morning," I spoke sipping on my wine.

"Morning doctor," Ali responded.

"Ali," I said with a grin.

"Keri don't start," Cree said looking my way.

"I'm not doing anything but sipping on my wine," I stated.

"Yeah okay," She responded.

"Cree let me get up on out of here, I'll call you later," He told her.

"Okay, let me walk you out," She replied.

I watched as he grabbed her hand as they walked out the kitchen, I heard them talking and her laughing at the front door before I finally heard it close. She walked back in the kitchen with the stupidest grin on her face, I couldn't do anything but laugh at her ass.

"Looks like someone had a real goodnight," I laughed.

"I did, I really did. We didn't do anything but talk and we fell asleep and he didn't even try anything. He was the perfect gentleman the whole night," She spoke.

"Aww Cree, that's what's up." I told her.

"Yeah he's nice. I like him," She admitted.

"Yay, I'm so happy for you girl, let's toast," I said raising my glass.

"You do know what time it is right?" She questioned laughing at me.

"It's five o' clock somewhere," I stated sipping more of my wine.

I grabbed the bottle and filled up my glass some more, and continue drinking.

"I'm going to make breakfast you want some?" She asked getting stuff out the fridge.

"I'm drinking mine," I responded holding up my glass.

"Okay, but I think you should slow down with the wine" She laughed.

"I will," I smiled taking another sip.

We talked and she told me all about her night with Ali as she cooked breakfast, it was so good to see her actually excited about a dude. I told her the right one would find her when the time was right and now look.

"So, what's going on with you Keri?" She asked looking at me.

"What are you talking about?" I replied not making eye contact.

"Please don't insult my intelligence Keri, I know you, just like you know me. I waited until you finished that whole bottle of wine so you could be nice and tipsy when I ask you, so spill it and don't make me ask you again," She threatened.

I took the rest of my glass to the head then took a deep breath before I told her what's been going on. I already felt the tears coming and I wasn't prepared to tell my sister my darkest secret.

"Cree, I need to tell you something," I started saying.

"Okay, what's up?" She stated looking at me.

I was feeling myself getting emotional and I didn't even start talking yet. I didn't know how I was going to tell my best friend that I was getting abused by my fiancé.

"What's up Keri, talk to me?" She said in a nervous tone.

"I haven't been completely honest with you, I need to tell you something and I don't know how to tell you," I started.

"Tell me what?" She asked getting impatient.

"I've been keeping a secret from you for a few years and I don't want you to be mad at me I thought I could handle it but as of lately it's starting to get out of control," I admitted.

"Keri, what the fuck is going on with you?" She exclaimed.

I took a deep breath and began telling her all about Max and I's relationship over the last few years. I told her all about the abuse and what happened the other night. I was so overwhelmed with emotion that I couldn't stop crying. It felt so good to finally tell her what I have been going through. I felt like complete shit for not telling her this sooner. By the time I was done we both had tears in our eyes.

"Keri," She mumbled through ears.

"I'm fine, really. I just wanted to finally tell you," I replied wiping my tears.

"This isn't fine Keri abuse is never fine, what the hell is wrong you for even staying with him after the first time he hit you? And why the fuck are you just telling me this shit anyway?" She questioned.

"I didn't want you to call me too weak for staying," I stated putting my head down.

"You still didn't answer my question, WHY THE FUCK ARE YOU STAYING WITH HIM KERI?" She yelled.

"He's paying for EVERYTHING with Khloe and my mom, without him I can't afford it all. Khloe needs this and you know it Cree," I told her.

"Keri baby listen to me and listen to me good, you can't help Khloe if your ass is dead. If you needed help you know I would have done anything in my power to help you and her, y'all are my family," She said crying.

"I know, I just don't know what to do anymore Cree, I don't want to live like this anymore," I admitted.

"Then leave baby, I will help you anyway I can, I promise you that," She said squeezing my hand.

"Okay," I replied nodding my head.

"Good, and after you leave I'm going get that nigga fucked up who the fuck do he think he is trying you like that like I won't bring the heat to his place," She said pissed off causing me to laugh.

"The heat Cree really? Stop watching them old ass shows please," I laughed through my tears.

"Come here girl, don't you ever in your life keep anything from me again or this friendship is over," She told me pulling me in for a hug.

"I promise I won't," I replied.

"Good," She responded kissing me on the cheek.

The rest of the day we sat and talked and decided that I would be leaving Max for good real soon. I was so thankful that Cree wasn't to mad at me for not telling her sooner, I really felt better that I told her. It was such a good feeling finally get this off my chest.

***

"Goodnight ladies," I greeted as I walked on to the hospital floor.

"Night Dr. Alexander, you have a patient that requested to see you as soon as you get in, they have been waiting all day and refused to see any doctor until you got on shift," The nurse told me.

"Well why wasn't I paged earlier?" I questioned getting mad.

"I'm just finding out myself when I got on shift," She replied.

"Okay thank you nurse," I responded.

I punched in and went straight into the patient's room to see what the issue was that they only wanted to see me. I knocked on the door before entering and when I walked in and saw Cobain laying in the bed flipping the channel on the television.

"What are you doing here?" I asked in a confused tone.

"Well hello to you doc, I've been waiting for you all day," He admitted.

"Why?" I questioned.

"Because I wanted to make sure you were good since I haven't heard from since you jumped out of a moving car," He joke making me smile.

"If I'm not mistaken the car wasn't moving, but I'm good thank you," I replied.

"Well I can see that," He said as he sat up in the bed looking at me.

"Well if you don't really need me I have to go start my shift," I spoke about to turn and walk out the door.

"Keri wait," He called out.

"Yes?" I responded.

"What's up with you?" He questioned.

"I just have a lot on my mind but I'll be good," I assured him.

"Leave with me," He suggested.

"I can't, I have work and patient's that need me here," I stated.

"I'll bring you back, just give me two hours," He requested holding up two fingers.

I stood there and thought about it for a second, a part of me wanted to say yes but the other part of me was telling me this was a bad idea and to stay my ass here and work but I was tired of always following the rules. So, against my better judgement I agreed to go with him.

"Fine two hours but then you have to bring me back because I really do have to work," I argued.

"I got you doctor," He replied with a smile.

"Let me get someone to cover my patients," I told him about to leave.

"That's already taken care of," He said causing me to stop in my tracks.

"HOW?" I questioned.

"I got a little pull, and I kinda figured you would have agreed to it so I paid someone to take care of shit while we were gone," He said with a shrug of his shoulders.

"Hmmm," I replied.

"Come Cinderella let's go so I can get you back before your chariot turns back into a pumpkin," He joked grabbing my hand and exiting out the room.

We left out the hospital hand in hand and got in his car and pulled off. I don't know what it was about him but being around him always made me feel comfortable. I felt protected and I haven't felt like that Max since the first year we started dating.

"Where are we going?" I questioned.

"Sit back and enjoy the ride beautiful," He told me.

I laid my head back and closed my eyes and just enjoyed the ride to wherever he's taking me. I found myself dosing off as he was driving the ride was so smooth.

"Wake up doctor we here," He said shaking me.

I opened my eyes and looked around and saw that we were at the beach.

"What are we doing here?" I asked rubbing my eyes.

"Chilling, come on," He said getting out the car.

I opened my door and got out the car and walked over to him while he held his hand out for me. I grabbed his hand and he pulled me close to him as we stated walking towards the boardwalk. The walk to the boardwalk was quiet at first and I was just enjoying being around him.

"So, Ms. Keri tell me what's on your mind, and before you lie and say nothing don't, I can read people very well and I'll know that you are lying and I don't like liars," He stated.

"I'm just thinking about life, all the shoulda, coulda, and wouldas, all the what if's," I admitted.

"Do you have any regrets?" He inquired.

"Yes and no, but the things I regret are just lessons learned," I spoke looking up at him.

"Interesting. I won't ask you about your regrets… not yet anyway but one day," He added.

"Do you have any regrets?" I threw back at him.

"Honestly… no I don't. I live my life how I want and everything I do is my choice," He spoke.

"Must be nice," I mumbled.

"Huh?" He asked.

"Oh nothing," I replied with a light smile.

We continued to walk and talk asking questions to each other back and forth, until we felt like we knew enough about at this moment.

"You're a very interesting man Mr. Wade," I stated.

"I hope that's a good thing," He replied.

"It could be," I laughed.

"Real shit doc, I know you have a situation at home but I'm feeling the fuck out of you, it's just something about you that I can't seem shake. I wake up in the morning just wanting to be in your presence even if it's just to watch you work," He admitted.

"Wow, I don't even know what to say," I spoke.

"It's cool doc, you don't have to say anything I just wanted to tell you what was on my mind," He added.

We walked a little further in silence both of us lost in our thoughts, once we got to the end of the boardwalk we looked over at the waves and just stood there.

"It's so peaceful out here," I spoke breaking the silence.

"Doc," He called out.

"Yes?" I replied looking at him.

He looked me in my eyes and grabbed the side of my face with his hand and caressed it then leaned down and kissed me. I haven't been kissed like this in so long, I reached up and put my arms around him as he passionately kissed me like it was our last time seeing each other. I pulled away and I don't know what came over me but I thought I should tell him about Max and I's relationship status.

"I'm leaving my fiancé," I admitted.

"What? Are you serious?" He questioned.

"Yes," I replied shaking my head up and down.

He picked me up and spun me around as he continued to kiss me all over my face.

"You just made my night doc," He said in between kisses causing me to throw my head back in laughter.

He put me down and as soon as he did my phone went off from the hospital, it was a page that read 911.

"I need to go back to work, I just got paged 911," I told him.

"Let's go," He responded grabbing my hand.

We got in the car and he sped all the way back to the hospital, I don't know what could possibly be going on for them to page me that there was an emergency especially since he paid someone to cover my shift. We pulled up to the hospital and I jumped out and ran inside straight to my floor and straight to the nurse's station.

"What happened? Who paged me?" I asked out of breath.

As soon as she was about to respond that's when I saw it, my little sister Khloe being rolled in on the gurney unresponsive.

Chapter 17- Cree

I can't believe the shit that Keri admitted to me, that shit left a sour taste in my mouth. I can't believe he was hitting her all this time and I never knew about it.

"What's on your mind babe? I've been calling your name for the last minutes and you didn't even hear me," Ali asked me pulling me from my thoughts.

"Oh, you were sorry, what were you saying?" I asked.

"I was asking what did you want to do today, but that can wait what's on your mind what has you so distracted?" He inquired.

I sat and thought if I should tell him what's going on with Keri and Max, I mean what's the worst that could happen. He could probably help more than me especially when it comes time to go pack up her stuff.

"Hello," He said waving his hand in front my face.

"Stop dammit," I replied slapping his hand down from my face.

"So, talk dam," He spoke sounding annoyed.

"I just found out some shit about my friend and it's really bothering the fuck out of me," I told him.

"Well since I've known you, I know you only have one friend. So, what's going on with the doctor?" He inquired.

"I shouldn't even be telling you this shit truthfully, I know I'm breaking all kinds of girl codes right now, but I know you could possibly help me," I said.

"What Cree. What's going on?" He asked again.

"Well Keri admitted to me that her fiancé has been beating on her," I admitted putting my head down.

"WHAT THE FUCK YOU MEAN HE'S BEEN BEATING HER?" He yelled.

"Just what I said, she told me it's been going on since he put that ring on her finger," I told him.

"Nah I know the doctor isn't that crazy to stay with a man that beats on her," He said shocked.

"She doesn't want to," I let him know.

"Well clearly, she does since she hasn't left him yet," He barked.

"Don't raise your voice at me Ali, I didn't do shit to you. I just found out myself. She can't leave him because she needs him and he knows that," I admitted.

"What the fuck you mean she needs him?" He questioned.

So, I started telling him the story of Keri, her mom and Khloe and where Max came into play at. I let him know the real deal and by the time I was done he was more pissed then from when I started.

"That's some real bitch nigga shit for real and he needs to get dealt with for real," He exclaimed.

"I know, I know," I said in a sad tone.

"Is she going to leave him?" He asked staring at me.

"That's what she said, we have plans to go over there this weekend to move her out," I told him.

"Well Cobain and I will be there with you guys just in case," He stated in a matter of fact tone.

"Okay," I replied.

"We going to take care of this shit, don't even worry about it. How is she holding up?" He asked concerned.

"She's fine, but she's always been like that. She's pretty strong so for her to finally admit this to me after all these years it must really be getting bad," I explained.

"Well she about to really be good," He stated.

I saw him pull out his phone and start texting, I could only bet that it was Cobain and he was telling him what I just told him. I hope Keri wouldn't be to mad at me for telling but something had to be done and Max had to be stopped.

"Don't worry about anything we got y'all and you know I definitely got you baby girl," He said kissing me on the tip of my nose.

"I know, I just don't want her mad at me," I told him giving him sad eyes.

"She won't, you just a concerned friend looking out for her," He said trying to make me feel better.

"Yeah, your right, I just hope she feels the same way,"

"She will, now what time do you have to be in the office today?" He asked changing the subject.

"At one," I told him.

"Okay well that leaves up with about three hours to do whatever you wanna do baby," He said looking at his watch.

As bad as I wanted to give in and give this sexy man my body I wasn't going to take it there with him yet. I wanted to make sure he was here for the right reasons, and I didn't want a repeat of my past experiences.

"Can you grease my scalp bae, I have my grease in my bag," I asked while trying to hold my laugh in.

"Hell, no last time I was walking around smelling like a coconut tree for days," He yelled making me laugh.

"First off don't do me and it wasn't that bad, your ass always over exaggerating," I said

in between laughter.

I was laughing so hard my stomach was hurting me, because he was dead serious. He called me cursing me out every day because he said he couldn't get the smell out is hands.

"The hell is wasn't, I had random ass people asking me if I just came from visiting an exotic island," He stated.

"Man whatever, let's just uber eat and chill," I suggested.

"Cool with me," I wasn't in the mood to be driving your ass around anyway," He looked at me and smirked.

"Shut up, what you want to eat?" I asked pulling out my phone.

"Whatever you want baby," He told me as he responded to a text on his phone.

"Okay," I responded.

This is the kind of stuff I enjoyed, we could go out and turn up together or stay home and chill together and still be good with each other's company. He walked over to me and I hopped on his back and he carried me to the living room then dropped me on the couch and started tickling me.

"STOPPPPPPPPPPPP," I yelled out trying to get away from him.

"Where are you going Cree?" He asked still tickling me.

"Okay, okay," I screamed.

"Okay what?" He teased.

"Okay big daddyyyyyy," I shouted then he stopped.

"That's what I thought," He smirked.

"Your such an asshole," I told him throwing a pillow at him.

"I'm your asshole though, so that's all that really matters to me," He stated.

"You better be,"

"Stay with me tonight," He said kissing me on my forehead, then my nose then finally my lips.

"I can't, I need to go home. I've been here with you every night that I forgot what my bed feels like," I responded.

"I know, but I enjoy you here with me," He stated.

"I enjoy being here with you too baby but I'm still going home," I said.

"Real shit Cree, ever since you been with me I haven't had any nightmares and I feel like that if you don't sleep with me they will return," He admitted.

"Aww babe why didn't you just say that then, I'll stay with you. I'll come right over after work," I replied kissing him.

"Thanks Cree," He said winking at me.

***

I pulled up to my job and was already to go home, I was in dire need of a nap and really didn't feel like being here but I had an appointment lined up and they have been calling all week to confirm. So, I had to do that but after that I was leaving. I'll just let my boss know I'm taking a half day.

"Hey Ming girl," I spoke walking into the office.

"Hey, your appointment called again to make sure y'all were still on," She told me shaking her head.

"Oh my god, that's so weird. How many times do we must confirm a date," I stated already annoyed with this client.

"Yeah tell me about it," She responded.

I walked into my office and closed the door, I dropped my bag on the chair and went and sat behind my desk and put my head down. Today was just one of them days where I just wanted to lay up with my boo and eat greasy food and chill. I couldn't wait until the day I become my own boss. I set my alarm and took a little cat nap until it was time for my appointment.

Soon as I felt myself dosing off my phone vibrates, I reached for it and saw that it was a text from Ali and instantly got a smile on my face.

Ali: *hope you got to wrk okay, since you didn't text me when you got there*

Me: *you so aggy bruh, I just got here not even ten minutes now*

Ali: *but your there*

Me: *Sorry babe dam*

Ali: *I'll see you later, hit me on your break*

Me: *yes babe*

I decided to finish up some designs that I had for a previous client until it was time for me to go, no need to waste time when I could do this and make the time speed up. I got so wrapped up in my design that I didn't even know Ming was calling me.

"Hey Cree, it's time to go," She reminded me.

"Thanks Ming," I replied never looking up.

I finished the last part of the design then gathered all my stuff and put it in my bag and got ready to go to meet this client. I grabbed the sticky note with the address and was on my way.

"Ming, I might be back," I told her heading out the door.

I got in my car and cut on music and luckily Future was already on the radio, so I got in trap mode then put the address in my GPS and made my way to the address. Thirty minutes later I was pulling up to a house, it looked like it needed a full makeover but that wasn't what I was here for I just only hoped the inside looked better than the outside.

I got out the car and headed towards the front door, I knocked and waited for someone to answer.

"Hello Cree, thank you for coming, I'm Dee," The man said introducing himself when he opened the door.

"Hello Dee, thanks for booking me," I replied as I walked into the house.

"It was my pleasure, you come highly recommended," He said.

"What did you want redesigned?" I asked pulling out my notepad.

"I wanted to turn my basement into my mancave," He told me.

"Okay, that I can definitely do for you Dee," I stated confidently.

"Good, right this way let me show you what you will be working with," He said as he led me to the basement.

I followed him through the house looking at it as I walked through it, it wasn't much of an improvement. If you ask me the whole needed to be thrown away and just start fresh. We got to a door in the kitchen that I'm assuming led to the basement. He opened the door and cut the lights on and went down the stairs, I followed behind him down the stairs, when we got downstairs I stopped in the middle of the room and did a full circle taking it all in.

"This is a nice size basement you have," I told him as I started drawing in my notebook

"Thanks, do you think you will be able to work with it?" He questioned.

"Absolutely," I replied.

I walked around the living room and took everything in as I sketched, this was going to be a big project but it could get done.

"Cree," He called.

"Yes," I replied still sketching.

"Who is Ali to you?" He asked making me look up and when I did I saw this look in his eyes that weren't there before.

"I don't know what you're talking about," I stated trying to make my way back to the steps.

I ran to the steps only to see someone else coming down them, I backed up and hit a wall.

"What do you want from me?" I cried.

"I want Ali, that's it," He admitted.

I knew I was good as dead if I stayed here, I needed to get out of here. I looked around and noticed a door at the other end of the room. I gathered up enough courage to try and make that run I counted to three and then took off running.

"HELP… HELP ME… PLEASE SOMEOMNE," I yelled running towards the door.

"Nobody can hear you Cree," I heard from behind me.

"Please, please don't hurt me," I cried.

"Don't worry it will all be over soon," Was the last thing I heard before I felt an electric current go through my body then it all went black.

Chapter18- Ali

Soon as Cree left I told Cobain to pull up so we could figure what the fuck we were going to do about this nigga Max and his hand problem. I already knew that if it was up to Cobain he was going to die. He was really feeling the doctor so I know shit was about to get real.

"Yo Ali where you at bro?" I heard Cobain call out as he walked in the house.

"In here," I yelled.

A few seconds later he was walking into my office with the pissed off face, so I already knew what was on his mind.

"Now run that shit by me again ol' girl told you," He stated soon as he walked in the room.

"I'm going to need for you to sit the fuck down bro all this pacing you doing isn't good for my carpets right now," I told him seriously.

"Shut the fuck up, and talk nigga dam, I'll buy your bougie ass a new fuckin' carpet," He replied with an annoyed tone.

"Fuck you," I replied.

"Ali real shit bro spill it," He stated.

I sat there and told him all the shit that Cree told me earlier, about the doctor and her fiancé. I didn't leave shit out.

"Are you fuckin' kidding me right now?" He yelled after I was done telling him.

"That was my same reaction when she told me too," I admitted.

"He has to die, simple as that," He spoke.

"We need to think rationally bro we can't just kill him and that's it," I tried to tell his hostile ass.

"Why the fuck not?" He challenged.

"We need to think smart, he comes from money. We can't just walk up to him and kill him, we need a plan," I explain.

"What did you find on this prick?" He asked ignoring my last statement.

I handed him the files I had sent over to me on anything my team could find on him, we both looked over everything trying to come up with a plan to get him.

"Man fuck this shit, I'm going to just put a bullet in his head when he's leaving work, I'll sit in the back of his car and wait until he gets in," He said closing the folder.

"Listen I'm going to need you to think logical and not with your emotions, I'm sure his car is surrounded my cameras and shit we need a REAL PLAN," I said slower for him to understand that I was serious.

"Figure that shit out then, and hurry the hell up. My trigger finger is itching and I need to release some pent-up frustration anyway," He spoke.

"I'm already on it," I admitted with a smirk.

We sat there devising a plan on how we were going to take this nigga down, it was going to take place sooner than later. Cobain was on a mission and this was one mission that he was going to enjoy being on.

"Have you seen any signs from her that she was home getting abused?" I asked.

I saw him thinking about it and then it looks like he had an ah ha moment then he spoke.

"Actually, one day we were chilling having a good and her phone rang and she got all jumpy and all of a sudden had to dip and was in a rush, and I couldn't understand it but now it's all making sense. Maybe it was that nigga calling her," He said as he thought back to that day.

"Dam," I mumbled.

"Exactly my point," He stated.

"Have you spoken to her?" I inquired.

"Nah not yet," He admitted.

"Well don't, not until you calm down anyway because I know you and you aint going to do nothing but scare her, and you know I'm right," I spoke.

"Yeah you right, but that nigga is good as dead," He stated.

"I already know," I chuckled.

I put the files on the desk and sat back and grabbed my phone off the desk, just as I picked it up it started to ring and I saw it was my baby Cree.

"Hey babe, you on break already?" I asked answering the phone.

"Hello Ali," I heard on the other end of the phone.

"WHO THE FUCK IS THIS AND WHERE THE FUCK IS CREE?" I barked jumping up.

When I jumped up so did Cobain he was watching and waiting for me to say something.

"Cree is such a beautiful woman Ali, you did a wonderful job with this one," He bragged into the phone.

"WHO THE FUCK IS THIS?" I barked.

"What a shame Ali that you don't know my voice, it's your old pal Dragon," He spoke so calmly.

"IF YOU HURT A HAIR ON HER HEAD I WILL FIND YOU, AND TOURTURE THEN KILL YOU AND YOUR ENTIRE FAMILY," I threatened.

"For someone who doesn't have the upper hand right now you are really talking a lot of shit," He spoke.

"MAN FUCK YOU, WHERE YOUR ASS. YOU TOUGH KIDNAPPING PEOPLE AN SHIT, TELL ME WHERE YOU AT FACE ME LIKE A FUCKIN' MAN YOU PUSSY," I Barked into the phone.

"In due time my friend, you killed someone near and dear to my heart and I think it's time for a little payback don't you think?" He asked.

"Dragon, I'm telling you know if I find you it's going to be a problem," I said through gritted teeth.

"I have to go but I'll be in touch, I'm going to have a little fun with my new friend here," He admitted.

"Ali? Please come get me, I'm scared," I heard Cree cry through the phone before the line went dead.

"FUCKKKKKKKK," I yelled tossing my phone against the wall making the screen shatter.

"What's going on bro?" Cobain questioned ready for action.

"Fuckkkkkk man, that was Dragon's ass he has Cree, talking 'bout payback for killing that nigga Bracka," I told him.

"We aint even kill that nigga his own people did when they came in their guns blazing and shit," Cobain said.

I sat in my chair leg shaking pissed off ready to go get my girl back. This shit was feeling like De Ja Vu and brought me back to a time I was working so hard to forget. One thing for certain and two things for sure the shit that happened with Ashanti wasn't going to happen with Cree and I put that on my life.

Chapter 19- Max

As I was sitting here looking at these pictures of Keri and this unknown man my fuckin' blood was boiling. I haven't seen her smile that bright in years but here she was showing all her got dam teeth. I don't know where we went wrong at, we were once so happy but now… now we were just here living together. We barely have sex unless I take it and I've been Cumming in her all this time and can't understand why her ass hasn't become pregnant yet.

I poured me another glass of alcohol, and took the whole glass back then slammed it down the table. The more liquor I drank the more upset I got at the fact that my fiancé was out here entertaining another dude. I knew that bullshit ass story about her leaving her phone in the car was a dam lie. Which is why I started having her followed and I was right with my suspicions.

I heard the front door open then close and I knew that Keri was finally home.

"KERI?" I called out.

She didn't reply, she just eventually walked into the room with a sad look on her face.

"What's wrong with you?" I asked.

"Khloe was rushed to the hospital I've been trying to call you and tell you," She said on the verge of tears.

"Mmmm, did she die?" I inquired.

"What no?" She came in unresponsive but they managed to save her," I stated.

"Did they now?" I replied in a shocked tone.

"What is wrong with you? Why are you acting like this my sister almost died and our sitting here acting you don't even care," She cried.

I walked over to the bar and poured myself another shot and took it back then turned around and faced her then threw the pictures at her.

"What is this?" She asked bending down to pick up the photos.

I watched her to see her reaction, her eyes got bright and she looked at me.

"You been following me?" She asked.

"That's what it seems now doesn't it?" I stated.

"But why?" She asked in a confused tone.

"WHY NOT KERI?" you out here acting like a little HOE," I yelled.

"I'm not doing anything, he's just a friend," She told me.

"A friend Keri since when? We've been together for five years and I have yet to meet this friend. So again, I ask a friend since when?" I screamed.

She looked at me and shook her head and tried to walk out the room, I ran after her and grabbed her arm and pushed her against the wall.

"What kind of friend do you kiss like this Keri?" I yelled shoving the picture in her face.

"Maxxxxx," She cried.

"Where the fuck do you think you're going Keri, I'm not done talking to you yet" I snapped raising my hand to slap her.

"Ahhhhhh Max," She screamed.

"Shut up, you are MY FINANCE and you out here acting like you common WHORE," I fumed.

"No, I'm not," She cried.

"NO? Then what do you call it huh tell me?" I demanded grabbing her by the face forcing her to look at me.

"Max I'm sorry, I just want to go back to Khloe," She sobbed loudly.

"You're so fuckin' ungrateful after all I do for you this is how you repay, what if I stop paying then what? Is that want you want?" I asked.

"Maxxxx pleaseeeeeeee," She cried.

"Max please what huh? You weren't saying Max please when you were out there smiling in the next man's face," I snapped tossing her to the floor.

I walked over to the bar and took another shot then I took off my belt and wrapped the buckle around my hand and came down across her legs.

"Owwwww Max," She screamed out.

I kept hitting her repeatedly with the belt all over her body. Not caring that she was crying.

"Max please stop I'm begging you," She cried in pain.

"I do so much for this family, I pay ALL the bills, I'm taking care of your mother and your sister and WHY? You know WHY BECAUSE I LOVE YOU AND THIS IS HOW YOU REPAY ME?" I yelled still hitting her with the belt.

Max please stop," She continued to cry out.

"You want to know something Keri? I knew that you weren't here with me for a long while now and I knew that I was losing you so that's why I did what I did, you left me no choice" I spoke in a drunken stupor.

"What are you talking about Max?" She asked through tears.

"I kept Khloe addicted to drugs, she's been clean, but when I felt me losing you I had to do something to keep you here. I knew you wouldn't leave me if Khloe was still sick because you needed me," I admitted.

"What?" She cried.

"SHUT UP THIS IS ALL YOUR FAULT," I yelled bringing the belt down on her again.

"AHHHHHHHHHHHHH," She screamed.

I started pacing around with my hands on my head, looking down at Keri on the floor crying hysterically.

"I've loved you since the day I saw your beautiful face Keri, you think I enjoy hitting you? I don't, I promise you I don't," I spoke.

I saw her trying to move and I didn't even stop her, she got on her knees and tried to crawl out the room. I stood up and walked over her and made her flinch, I kept walking past her and down the steps leaving her there alone battered.

Chapter20- Cobain

The shit with Cree was fuckin' crazy as fuck, I don't know how the fuck he managed to snatch her like that. Ali was going crazy to find her so that history won't repeat itself. He didn't tell me but I knew that was the reason he never got close to a female after Ashanti, then when he finally decided to take a leap of faith this shit happens so I know it was really fuckin' with him the long way.

I was on my way to meet one of my techs to see if we could get a trace on Cree's phone, then I was going to her job to talk to anyone to see if they know where this meeting was taking place. Ali mind was on murder so I had to leave him behind because he was working with emotions right now and emotions get you killed.

I had to push shit with Keri on the backburner until we brought Cree home, I didn't even want to tell her no shit like this. She didn't need any more stress on her, her and

Cree are to close and something like this would break her and I couldn't look after her and Ali and get shit done. I pulled up alongside of another car.

"What's good homie?" I spoke rolling the window down.

"Can't call it, what you got for me?" He asked getting right to the point.

I tossed him the phone along with an envelope.

"I need a trace done on the last number that called that phone. Whatever you can find I don't care what it is just let me know," I stated.

"I got you, what the hell happened to it?" He asked.

"You know Ali got anger issues," I joked.

"That he does," He chuckled.

"So, whatever you find out just hit my line until we can get Ali another phone," I told him.

"Aight, I got you," He spoke.

"ASAP, this is state of emergency big," I insisted.

"Copy, give me a little while and I'm going to be in touch" He replied pulling off.

My next stop was her job, I know they must keep some kind of records of when they staff go out to meet clients or some shit. My phone rang and I saw it was Ali calling from his office phone.

"Anything yet?' He asked soon as I picked up.

"Nah, not yet. You already know that as soon as I hear something you going to be the first person I call," I told him.

"Yeah, I know, I just feel so useless right now, a nigga doesn't feel right just sitting home pacing the fuckin' floor while you out putting in the footwork," He admitted.

"Nah you good son, you know I got you. Besides you already don't have it all up there so I'm just trying to save the world from seeing the monster that I know you are dying to let out," I stated.

"I hear you bro, but that's my shorty out there," He acknowledged.

"I know that and that's what I'm here for to help you, as soon as I find out anything I'll holla at you. In the meantime, get someone to bring your hostile ass a new phone," I joked.

"Yeah that's a good idea," He laughed.

"I'll be in touch," I said.

"Aight," He replied hanging up.

I pulled up to her job and hopped out and started knocking on the door but nobody came to the door. That's when I saw the sign that said they were gone for the rest of the day.

"FUCKKKKKKKK, this can't be happening right now," I yelled out frustrated.

I jumped back in my car and sat there for a minute, I didn't know where to go now, I had nothing to do until my man got back to me with the phone trace. So, shit was pretty much on standstill right now. I heard my phone ringing and saw that it was Keri and started not to pick up because I didn't want to have to lie to her or have her get my mind fucked up.

I don't play that hitting shit and if I found out before I probably would have stopped fuckin with her after I killed that nigga that was hitting her. I was in my feelings because she was smarter than that, but I guess when your back is against the wall you do a lot of shit you aint proud of.

"Wassup Keri, I'm a little busy right now and can't talk," I told her as soon as I answered the phone.

"Cobain can you come get me please?" She said in a low tone.

"Come get you? where are you? What happened?" I asked in a panic tone.

"I'm home and I'm alone and scared. I need you," I heard her cry through the phone.

"Keri calm down baby and tell me what happened," I stated in a calmer tone.

I didn't want to upset her more then she already was, so I calmed myself down and spoke softer.

"I'm on my way Keri, just text me your address and I promise I'm on my way. You can tell me when I get there," I insisted.

She was crying so bad that I couldn't understand what she was telling me, I waited until I received the text and put her address in my GPS and did 100 MPH all the way there. I was shocked I didn't get pulled over as fast as I was driving. The GPS said forty minutes from my current location and I made to the address that she sent me in about twenty-five minutes. When I got to the house I jumped out the car leaving it running and pulled my gun out and made my way to the door.

I knocked and waited but didn't hear anything, I turned the knob and it was unlocked I pointed my gun in the house and slowly walked inside. I wasn't familiar with this house so I had to walk through the house looking for Keri. I didn't know what I was walking in on so I didn't want to scream her name out. I heard some moaning coming from upstairs so that's where I headed next.

"Keri?" I called out.

"In here," She weakly responded.

When I got to where she was she was laying on the floor looking fucked up. I ran over and kneeled beside her.

"Keri what happened to you?" I asked trying to pick her up without causing her pain.

That's when I looked around and noticed the photos of us spread out on the bedroom floor.

"What the fuck is this?" I asked looking at all the different pictures of us from when we were at the boardwalk.

I picked her up and she cried in my arms.

"I'm sorry, I'm trying to be as gentle as possible," I told her.

I was trying my best to control the anger that was boiling inside of me, I couldn't wait to get my hands on this guy and kill him with my bare hands.

"Where did he go Keri?" I asked.

"He left," She replied weakly.

"I need you to tell me what happened," I insisted.

She began telling me how when she came home she was confronted by him with pictures then he started beating her with the belt then after he was done he walked out leaving her there alone.

"Okay, don't even worry about it I got you, I'm going to get you out of here," I told her.

"Thank you, Cobain," She said through tears.

I carried her slowly down the steps as she silently cried in my chest. Hearing her crying was doing something to my manhood, I was pissed that she even had to go through this shit. Once we got to the front of the house I instantly stopped when I came face to face with a gun, but what was confusing me was the person that was holding the gun.

"Shyne what the hell are you doing here?" I barked.

"Is this the friend that you told my daughter that you wanted her to meet one day?" She asked with tears falling from her eyes.

"This isn't the time or the place for us to be having this conversation Shyne," I yelled.

"That's the problem it's never the right time or place for us to EVER have this conversation Cobain," She yelled pointing the gun between the both of us.

"Can you stand?" I asked Keri.

She nodded her head up and down, so I slowly placed her down on her feet and leaned her up against the wall.

"YOU SEE HOW YOU ARE SO LOVING AND GENTLE WITH HER, WHY CAN'T YOU BE LIKE THAT WITH ME? I HAVE ALWAYS LOVED YOU," She screamed.

I slowly walked towards her with my hands up because I didn't want to make the mistake of scaring her then the gun goes off.

"Shyne listen to me, we go through this all the time. You are the mother of my daughter nothing more, nothing less. We are co-parenting Kaylee that's it," I stated.

"NO… NO… that's not it. I do everything you ask of me, I cook, clean, I suck your dick and fuck you whenever you want. I haven't had a man since I had Kaylee," She explained.

"Shyne you chose to do those things, they were never forced but at the same time I made sure you never wanted for anything. As for dating you could have been had a man, YOU chose not to get one," I reasoned with her still getting closer.

"I don't want any of that, all I wanted was you, I love you for you not for what you can do for me," She cried.

I looked back at Keri mad that she even had to hear all this shit and that I had placed her in a fucked-up situation. I looked back at Shyne and when she wiped the falling tears I used that as my chance to try and take the gun from her. I grabbed her wrist and tried to take the gun from her we wrestled for a minute because she had a grip on the gun.

"Let me gooooooo Cobain," She shouted.

"POP" Was all that was heard when the gun went off.

"NOOOOOOOOOOOO," I heard Keri yell.

TO BE CONTINUED….

Made in the USA
Lexington, KY
13 November 2019